Fiction

COUNTDOWN BUTTERFLY

R.R. RAITA

Copyright © 2024 R.R. RAITA

All rights reserved

The characters and events portrayed in this book are fictitious. Any similarity to real persons, living or dead, is coincidental and not intended by the author.

No part of this book may be reproduced, or stored in a retrieval system, or transmitted in any form or by any means, electronic, mechanical, photocopying, recording, or otherwise, without express written permission of the publisher.

ISBN: 9798303432529

I want to dedicate this book to my family and friends.

"The virtuous man contents himself with dreaming that which the wicked man does in actual life."

-SIGMUND FREUD

CONTENTS

Title Page

Copyright

Dedication

Epigraph

Prologue

AnxiEty	1
Royal Flush	51
Limbo	159
ABOUT THE AUTHOR	176

PROLOGUE

Alex walks inside The Savoy using the umbrella as a walking cane and goes straight to the reception.

"Hi, is my room ready?"

"Yes, sir, as requested, we have sent a bottle of champagne to your room."

"Thanks."

"If you need anything else, please let us know."

"Will do."

Alex takes the elevator up to room 108, goes inside, drops the umbrella on the floor, and pours himself a glass of champagne. Then he hears a soft knock on his door. He opens it and sees a gorgeous redhead woman wearing a black leather skirt and boots with a leopard top. The gorgeous redhead is none other than Larry Gold's wife. Alex looks her up and down.

"You are late."

"Well, good things deserve the…"

"Come in and shut the door."

Alex turns his back on her and goes back into the room. She pauses for a moment, surprised by Alex's rude behaviour, but she nevertheless follows him inside. Alex leans back against the wall, sipping his champagne.

"I could use a drink."

"The bottle is over there; help yourself."

Alex points at the champagne bottle.

"A gentleman will have poured a drink for me too."
She pours a glass for herself, then turns around, looking back at Alex with fire in her eyes.

"I never claimed to be a gentleman."
Alex starts an eye-starting contest with her determined not to lose whatever the cost.

"You know my husband is looking for you all over London."

"I know." Alex, unfazed, takes a sip of champagne.

"I wonder what will happen if he finds us here."

"There will be blood."

"Yours or his?"

"Call him and find out."

"So, you are some sort of gangster?"

"No, I'm not."

"What then?"

"I am the beast."

"The beast?"

"Yeah, the beast."

Alex recites The Beast poem.

The Beast

My temper animalistic

Driven by instinct.

Feeding on passion

Devoted to sin.

Ready to devour,

Every day, every hour

The blood in your veins

Live and die in vain.

ANXIETY

Late at night in London, a dark grey Volkswagen Passat pulls up and parks in Soho Square Gardens. The driver wears a blue shirt and jeans. He is in his late 30s and has short dark hair, brown eyes, and a clean shave with a scar on his upper lip. He turns off the engine and goes on his Uber app.

"Let's see, Alex, what's your rating, 4.8? What!? It was four-point nine yesterday, and I bet it's because of that prick that I helped him with his bags eventually. What more did he want?"

Alex steps out of the car and stretches a bit.

"My back is killing me," he says while looking around.

Soho Square is quiet and peaceful, with no one in sight. The building lights illuminate the pavement and part of the street while the garden is engulfed in darkness. Soho Square Gardens, this small patch of nature is surrounded by a metal fence; this little fortress is under siege by the army of concrete buildings and city lights. King Charles II's statue stands tall in the centre of the garden like a general determined to protect this small patch of heaven at all costs.

Alex goes back into his car, locks the doors, and leans back on his chair.

"Time to take a break," he says, closing his eyes. Out of nowhere, a man appears, wondering about. The Volkswagen catches his eye as the internal lights from the car turn off slowly. He approaches the car from the passenger side and sees Alex resting. The stranger starts knocking on the window.

"Hey, let me suck your dick," says the stranger.

"What!?" Alex jumps up from his chair as he opens his eyes.

"Let me suck your dick," he says again.

"What!? No, go away, bro," Alex replies to the man.

"C'mon on, let me suck your dick,"

"No, bro, go away!"

"Let me suck your dick."

"Go away!" Alex screams.

"Let me suck your dick, let me suck your dick, let me suck your dick."

"What the hell is wrong with you? Go away!"

"Let me suck your dick, let me suck your dick, let me suck your dick."

"I'm driving away now!" Alex shouts back at him as he starts the car and drives away. Then his phone rings. It's his friend Dan, who is also an Uber driver.

"Hey Alex, how's it going?"

"Like shit, bro."

"I told you, Central London sucks."

"I didn't know you meant literally."

"What?" Dan exclaims.

"Bro, there was this guy just a moment ago who wanted to suck me off."

"What, are you serious?"

"Yeah, bro, he was banging on my window and kept

saying let me suck your dick."

"Wow, that's crazy, man," Dan says surprisingly.

"Yeah, he really pissed me off. I stopped in Soho Square to take a break, and then I saw this lunatic banging on my window."

"You seem stressed; maybe you should have let him do it." Dan starts laughing.

"Fuck off!"

"Hey, no one needs to know. I know one driver who was offered £100 for a blowjob."

"To give one or to get one?"

"I don't know, but 100£ is 100£."

"Oh, I see it was you. Ha, Ha!" Alex says while laughing out loud.

"No man, some guy I know."

"Yeah, right, let me see your wallet. I bet there is 100£ in there."

"Dickhead."

"Okay, okay, let's say I believe you."

"You should do the airport only just like me, come and join the queue."

"I don't know. I'll stay here with the "sex zombies" for a while," Alex replies.

"Be careful; they might get you in the end –"

"What is this guy doing?"

"What?"

"Some asshole just cut me off."

"See, you don't get that at the airport, no drunk people, no drama, and no "sex zombies.""

"Yeah, you just sit around for ages waiting."

"It's great, it's like fishing."

"I hate fishing."

"It's 2015. It's high-tech fishing with a

smartphone, and you have Facebook, Instagram, and Netflix. It's almost like you're sitting at home on your sofa."

"You are so lazy."

"Look who's talking. This is the thanks I get for saving you from that factory. Go back then."

"I'm not going back to that sandwich factory; I can't stand them anymore; even when I see sandwiches in the store, I'm like, eh…"

"What are you talking about? They were good. I liked the ones with the ham and cheese that you used to steal and brought back home."

"I didn't steal them; I bought them for half the price, which was the only perk of working in that cold factory."

"Speaking of food, barbeque at my place this weekend. Are you in?" Dan asks.

"Not sure."

"Why not? Now, you don't like barbecues also. What kind of man are you?"

"It's not that I don't like barbecues. I have to work this weekend, and I need the money."

"Come on, Alex, you always have to work."

"I have to do the MOT and a doctor's appointment."

"Is everything okay?"

"Yeah, the car is fine; it purrs like a cat."

"I'm talking about you, Jackass."

"Yeah, I'm good. It's just a checkup."

"Okay, if you die, can I get the Volkswagen?"

"No, I'm taking it to my grave. HA! HA!" Alex laughs loudly.

"Seriously, can we switch cars?"

"We have the same car."

"Yes, but mine is one year older and has more miles on."

"And you paid more for it, dumbass."

"Hey Jackass! I bought it like two years before you did."

"What can I say? You rush, you lose."

"You're going back to Romania this summer?"

"I'm not sure; the flights are expensive during summer. Maybe I will go in September or October."

"I'm going in August.."

"When is the most expensive? What did you do to win the lottery?"

"No man, I'm driving there. I have a spare seat if you want to come. We can chip in for petrol, and it's good to have another driver."

"I might take you up on that offer –"

"Damn, got to go, Alex. I just got a bite; looks like a big trip, 50 minutes plus, now that's what I call a 'whale.'"

"Oh, nice one, take care."

"Okay, see you, bro."

Alex is standing outside a small office building, hesitating to go inside. Next to the entrance on the upper right-side wall, there is a sign, Dr. Kingsley Linwood Psychiatrist. Alex takes a deep breath, opens the door, and walks inside. On the right is a small waiting area with a few empty chairs and a coffee table covered with magazines. On the left wall are two big windows, natural light illuminating the office. There is a receptionist desk in front, and next to it on the left side is a wooden door with Doctor Kingsley Linwood written on a metal plate. Above the wall behind the receptionist's desk is a painting of an old ship sailing on a calm sea. The receptionist, a blonde girl with a beautiful smile, greets Alex.

"Hi, I'm Linda; how can I help you?"
"Hi, I have an appointment at 1 pm."
"Okay, and your name, please?"
"Alex Raita."
"Okay, Mr. Alex, have a seat. Doctor Kingsley will be with you shortly. Can I get you anything, water, tea?"
"No, thanks."

Alex sits with his arms crossed around his chest,

glancing over the magazines on the table, but nothing catches his eye. His right leg twitches involuntarily as time passes by. Alex takes a moment to admire the painting on the wall, hoping it will calm him down, and glances out the window from time to time at the people walking by. But nothing seems to work, and his leg is twitching faster and faster by the second. He can't take it anymore and decides to run away and cancel the whole thing. Alex stands up, and at the same time, Doctors' Kingsley door opens, and a patient comes out. Alex froze for a moment, then jumped back down on his chair. His right leg starts twitching again. The patient walks out the door, followed closely by Doctor Kingsley, a tall sixty-year-old white man with grey hair and spectacles, wearing a beige cardigan with a blue shirt, blue jeans, and brown shoes. After saying goodbye to his patient, doctor Kingsley walks up to Alex and notices his leg twitching and stiff body language.

"Hi, you must be Alex Raita. I'm Doctor Kingsley Linwood. It's nice to meet you," he says as he extends his arm to Alex.

"Hi, Doctor. It's nice to meet you too." Alex stubbles as he gets up and shakes his hand.

"Did I say your last name, right? Sorry if I didn't. I have never heard that name before," Doctor Kingsley apologises.

"No, you were very close. It's a Romanian name."

"Romania, I was at a wedding there last year in Bucharest, which was very nice. I loved the food; what was that dish called sar…"

"Sarmale."

"Sarmale, that's the one. It's very nice, sarmale and palinca."

"You remember palinca?"

"Yes, because it almost killed me."

Doctor Kingsley places his hand on his chest and smiles at Alex.

"Well, it's not for the weak." Alex smiles back.

"Hey, I'm not as young as you, but I can still hold my own, more or less."

"My grandpa is 72 years old and has a shot of palinca every morning, noon, and evening."

"Dear God!? And I thought that I was brave enough to survive one day."

"What can I say? Romanians are built differently."

"No arguments there. I've seen it with my own two eyes. Please join me in my office."

As they pass the receptionist's desk, Doctor Kingsley turns toward Linda.

"Linda darling, can you bring us some tea? Do we have any more of those biscuits?"

"Yes, sure, doctor be with you in a sec –"

"It's okay, but you don't have to…"

Alex interrupts their conversation.

"Please, it's no trouble at all. I know nothing can compare to palinca."

Doctor Kingsley places his hand on Alex's shoulder.

"Let's have a tea party instead."

Alex and Doctor Kingsley walk into a small room with a large window on the left wall. A small desk on the right side with Doctor Kingsley's diploma hanging on the wall above the desk. In the centre of the room are two leather chairs opposite each other. Each chair has a small table on the right side.

"Please have a seat." Doctor Kingsley pointed at the chairs.

"I will join you shortly, just getting my notebook."

Alex takes a seat on the first chair with his back against the door, again with his arms crossed around his chest. Linda walks in with a tray with two cups of tea and biscuits and places them on each side table of the chairs. And then swiftly walks out.

"Thank you, Linda."

Doctor Kingsley whispers softly as he adds a new entry to his notebook.

"Thank you," Alex's response comes in too late as Linda closes the door behind her. Doctor Kingsley takes a seat in front of Alex and takes a sip of tea.

"Linda makes the best tea ever; you should try it." Doctor Kingsley points out the teacup beside Alex. Alex reaches out and accidentally spills the cup.

"Shit! I'm sorry."

"No worries, Alex, it happens."

Doctor Kingsley grabs a few tissues from his desk and cleans the table.

"I'm so sorry, doctor, I'm –"

"No worries, it's fine, Alex. Please call me Kingsley."

"I always do like this; I'm so clumsy."

"Really, it's fine; there is nothing to worry about."

Doctor Kingsley cracks open the door.

"Linda darling, can we get another tea, please?"

Doctor Kingsley sits back down. Alex is looking down at the floor, embarrassed by the situation. Linda brings another tea and walks out without saying anything.

"Thank you," Alex whispers as Linda closes the door behind her.

"How are you, Alex?"

"Good, I guess."

Alex is still staring at the floor.

"Alex, look at me," Doctor Kingsley speaks in a calm and assertive manner. Alex raises his head and makes eye contact with Doctor Kingsley.

"I'm not here to judge you, okay?"

Doctor Kingsley carries on with a calm and assertive tone.

"Have you ever been in therapy before?" Doctor Kingsley asks.

"No, this is my first time," Alex replies.

"I see."

Doctor Kingsley makes an entry in his notebook.

"As I mentioned before, I am not here to judge you. I'm here to listen to you, give you my undivided attention, and help you deal with whatever you are going through. Just take a moment and let that sink in. We can talk whenever you feel ready, or we can enjoy the silence together. This is your time, and you decide how to spend it, okay? Take a deep breath and relax; this is a safe space."

Alex nods his head, takes a deep breath, and then stares back at the floor. After a few moments, he opens his arms and takes on a more relaxed position.

"I think I suffer from anxiety, social anxiety," Alex starts.

"What makes you say that?"

"I don't feel comfortable around people. I feel anxious."

"How long have you been feeling this way?" Doctor Kingsley asked.

"Most of my life, I've always been a bit shy, more

of an introvert, especially in my early school years, but I think over time it got worse."

"There is nothing wrong with being an introvert."

"I don't want to be like that anymore. I don't want to feel nervous around people. I don't want to be different anymore."

"I understand, but you will be surprised to know that anxiety and stress are common these days. A large majority of the population suffers from anxiety or stress. You are not as different as you may think you are. However, people deal with these issues differently. Some are more reserved and quieter, and some tend to use jokes to hide their anxiety; others tend to talk a lot when they feel nervous or anxious," Doctor Kingsley explained.

"Really!? I always thought that those people were more confident than I am."

"Confident people get more involved in the conversation or, in some cases, dominate the conversation. However, body language is what gives them away. Here is a little tip for you: next time you feel different, study the body language of people around you. Confident people have a strong body posture and tend to keep their chin up, chest forward, and eye contact when speaking. On the other hand, anxious people keep their chin slightly down and shoulders up and struggle to maintain eye contact. Also, they are a bit clumsy, and we all are sometimes, but, in their case, it happens more often, and they are unsure of their actions."

"Like I did a moment ago, spilling the tea. Damn, I had no idea. Now that I think about it, I am always clumsy, so that's why."

"It depends. It can be a sign of anxiety, but it is not a rule. Try not to focus on it too much. Tell me, what was your childhood like?"

"Why?" Alex asks.

"It could be relevant to identify the root of your anxiety."

Alex takes a defensive body stance, crossing his arms around his chest again.

"My childhood was normal, I guess…"

"How do you define a normal childhood?" Doctor Kingsley asks.

"I don't know, and like any other regular family, you got good days and bad days. I don't know what you want me to say?"

"Did you experience any trauma or abuse?"

"No, not really…"

"Did your parents ever hit you?"

"My dad beat us once when we were small." Alex clears his throat.

"When you say we, who do you mean?"

"Oh, me and my brother, but we did something stupid; we deserved it."

Doctor Kingsley adds a note in his journal.

"How did your father hit you with his hands or belt or something else?"

"With a belt, but like I said, it's nothing, I know tons of people who got their ass kicked every week by their parents. So, my brother and I were very lucky that it happened only once. That's just the way things are in Romania. Like I said, it was a normal childhood," Alex tried to explain himself again.

"Any other incident or abuse that you can think about?"

"Nope."

"Abuse can also be verbal, sexual, or psychological. Did you experience anything like that?"

"No." Alex's leg starts twitching again as he pulls back in his chair.

"Okay, then let's move on. How is your current situation? Tell me a bit about yourself."

"What do you want to know?" Alex asks.

"What do you do for work?"

"I'm an Uber driver."

"How is that? Do you enjoy it?"

"It's good, I guess; you have good and bad days, but overall, it's good. I enjoy not having a boss or a supervisor or someone nagging you. Plus, I set up my own schedule. You know, I work when I want; if I want to go on holiday, I just go, and I don't have to ask for permission."

"That sounds like a pretty good gig."

"It is, can't complain so far."

"How did you come by it? Did you see an ad?" Doctor Kingsley asks.

"Oh, a friend of mine recommended it. He started before me, and he sort of talked me into it."

"What about your social life? I know you said about social anxiety, but do you have a few close friends with whom you interact?"

"I have one or two."

"Do you go out with them? Do you hang out, maybe?"

"Sometimes we go to a pub. I'm okay when it's a one-to-one thing, but I usually say no when more people are involved. I have a friend that I visit sometimes, and he always invites me when he throws a party or barbeque; that's when I usually make up an excuse not to go."

"What about your brother? Are you two close?"

"Yeah, we talk all the time over the phone."

"Is he here in London?"

"No, he's back home in Romania."

"Do you go back home to visit your family or not that often?"

"Yeah, I go twice maybe three times a year."

"How do you feel when you go back?"

"Good. I look forward to spending time with my brother and family."

"What about your love life? Do you have an intimate partner?"

"What, do you mean like a girlfriend?"

"Yes, girlfriend, boyfriend?"

"No, I'm single. No girlfriend," Alex says.

"What was the longest relationship that you had?"

"I... never had a relationship."

Doctor Kingsley adds another note in his journal.

"Why do you think that is happening?"

"I think because of my anxiety, when it comes to women, it's even worse, I can't talk to women. I mean, I can talk with them about random stuff like the weather, but I can't ask them out on a date, and I get really nervous."

"I see." Doctor Kingsley adds another entry in his journal. "Do you exercise and go to the gym?" Doctor Kingsley continues with his questions.

"I go to the gym a few times a week."

"That's good. Exercise is recommended for anxiety

and depression."

"Any hobbies? What do you do when you want to relax?"

"Go for a walk and listen to music. Get my headset on and go."

"Where do you go?"

"Nowhere in particular, just close to my home. On the main road, there are trees planted on the pavement, and in the middle of the road, the two lanes are divided into green areas with trees planted in the middle."

"That sounds nice," says Doctor Kingsley.

"It is especially during summer, and it looks great."

"What music do you listen to? Do you have any specific genres?"

"I listen to Hip-Hop and R&B."

"I personally don't listen to Hip-Hop, but I'm not sure that is classified as calm music; perhaps I'm mistaken."

"It depends; some songs can be, or some rappers are, let's say, less aggressive."

"Just for the record, I'm not against hip-hop or any other music genre. I wouldn't recommend any music or activities that raise your anxiety levels. If this genre helps reduce your anxiety, carry on," explains Doctor Kingsley.

Alex takes a sip of tea.

"Can I ask you something in return?" Alex asks.

"Definitely," replies Doctor Kingsley.

"Have you treated anyone like me before?"

"I don't discuss my patients, doctor-patient confidentiality. But I have treated people with anxiety before, if that's what you are wondering."

"Is there any hope for me?"

"Of course."

"So, what's the first step in fixing this?"

"You already took the first step by coming here. Second, to paraphrase you, we can fix this, but it's not going to be an easy fix since you have experienced anxiety for so many years. I will prescribe you some medication and a visit once a week. Also, you can use some positive affirmations like, "I am powerful and confident. Whatever happens, I can handle it." I want you to repeat this phrase every morning and night before going to bed or whenever you feel anxious."

"Is that once-a-week visit necessary? Aren't the medication and affirmation enough?"

"Am I such a bad host?" Doctor Kingsley smiles at Alex.

"No, that's not what I meant; I was just wondering what we will talk about for one hour."

"We can talk about whatever. The objective of these visits is to see how you are doing and track your progress. Discuss any issue in your life or any challenges that you might face. Also, to come up with a strategy to overcome your anxiety, more suited to your needs."

"Okay, I guess that makes sense."

"Now I have two openings, one on Tuesday at 2 pm and the other on Friday at 10 am. Which one works best for you?"

"Tuesday, on Friday, I usually sleep at that hour. I tend to work on the weekend nights."

"Great, I will see you Tuesday then," says Doctor Kingsley as he looks at his wristwatch.

"And we are done for today. Looking forward to our next session."

"Thank you so much. See you next time."

"This is your prescription; you should be able to find this medication at any pharmacy."

Doctor Kingsley hands the prescription to Alex as both get up from the chairs and head towards the exit.

"See you next time."

"Take care, Alex."

"Bye, have a good day."

Linda raises her head over the desk, smiling at Alex as he walks out the door.

As he drives through London late at night, Alex gets a trip request on his Uber App and accepts it.

"Let's see what we have here... Laura, 3.5 stars. Damn, what did you do, Laura?"

After driving for a few minutes, Alex pulls up to Laura's location.

Laura is a 25-year-old brunette with blue eyes. She gets in his car.

"Hi, are you my driver, Alex?"

"Hi, yes."

"Great, take me home."

"That's the job…"
"So, how was your night, Alex?"
"Not too bad. Yours?"
"Great, I went to this party."
"Nice, did you have a good time?"
"Yes, too bad it ended. I still feel like partying, you know."
"Well, every party ends sooner or later."
"But I don't want it to end, you know. Do you like to party, Alex?"
"Sometimes."
"Maybe you and I can party."
"Maybe on my days off."
"Why not tonight?"
"Tonight? I'm working tonight," says Alex.
"So, what? Just take the night off."
"Sorry, I can't."
"Why not? I mean, you are your own boss. You can do whatever."
"I still have to pay rent," replies Alex.
"Oh, come on, we can get some coke, go back to my place, and party."
"No, I'm sorry, miss, I can't."
"Yes, you can, and call me Laura."
"Sorry, Laura, but no."
"Can you at least get me some coke?"
"No, sorry, I don't know anybody."
"Come on, sure you do; you must know someone."
"No, I don't."
"Come on, you are an Uber driver, so you surely have someone."
"I'm an Uber driver, not a drug dealer."
"You are not fun at all, you know."

"Yeah, I know."
Alex stops the car.
"We are here, and this is your house."
Alex points out the window at a red brick house.
"Come on, last chance."
"No, sorry."
"Come on, do you want me to beg?"
"No, that's not it."
"Come on, seriously, let's get some coke, and you can do to me whatever you want."
"No, sorry, please go."
"Seriously, you are turning me down. What's wrong with you? Are you gay?"
"No, that's not it. Please go."
"Then you are just really dumb; it's no wonder you are an Uber driver."
"Seriously, now, please go."
"Whatever, go back to your shit job, you fucking loser!" Laura gets out of the car and slams the door behind her.
"Okay, now I know why you have a 3.5 rating. I need a break."
Alex turns off his Uber app as he drives away. A few moments later, he receives a phone call from his friend Dan.
"Hey, let me suck your dick."
"Ha, Ha! Hi, you bastard," Alex says jokingly.
"Come on, man, let me suck your dick."
"Oh, shut up, bro."
"Ha, Ha! I'm still laughing about that every time."
"I'm glad you are enjoying yourself asshole."
"Hey now, how come I'm the bad guy?"
"I don't know, but you are."

"How are you? Still working in London, or should I say zombie land."

"Yeah," Alex replies.

"Hey, dumb ass! When are you finally going to wake up and join me at the airport?"

"Never, how is that?"

"Fine by me. Better if you stay in London. Who knows, if you come to the airport, the "sex zombies" might follow you."

"Very funny, what can I say?"

"So, how is London? Is it still busy, still weird?"

"Yes, and yes. Feels like I'm in that game GTA. I just got another weird one a minute ago."

"Ha, Ha! I knew it."

"You cold-hearted bastard, you are enjoying this."

"Fuck yeah. Come on, let's hear it."

"Oh, I got this girl just a moment ago who wanted to do coke. She was asking me to get cocaine and go back to her place to party."

"Bro, really!?"

"Yeah."

"And?"

"Nothing. I dropped her off and drove away."

"Oh man, how can you turn that down?"

"Easy, I don't do drugs."

"So what?"

"What do you mean so what?"

"Man, I'm so disappointed in you."

"Fuck off, I'm not having sex with a drugged-up girl."

"Why not?" Dan asks.

"What do you mean why not? Are you insane?"

"Man, girls who do cocaine really like to party, if

you know what I mean."
"No, thanks."
"Man, you are so stupid."
"Fuck off."
"I'm ashamed to call you my friend anymore. You don't like dudes, you don't like girls, what's the matter with you?" Dan asks.
"Bro, you lost your mind. How can I do that? I was already picturing the headline: Uber Driver drugs passenger and rapes her," Alex replies.
"Man, you are overreacting."
"Fuck that, bro. I don't want to risk it."
"No risk, no reward."
"Yeah, more like no risk, no jail."
"You don't like to have fun at all, do you?"
"Yeah, I do."
"So why didn't you show up to my party then?"
"Well..."
"Ha-Ha! Got you."
"Well, I was busy."
"Sure, you were. Stop lying, man."
"I'm not lying, I was–"
"Stop it, man, I don't buy it."
"Yeah, well, whatever, goodbye then."
"Come on, don't be like that. You are always working, which is not good for you, man, so you should take a break sometimes. Come and hang out, have a beer, and relax a bit, you know," Dan tries to convince him.
"Maybe next time."
"I'm having another party in two weeks. Bring your ass over, okay."
"Maybe, we'll see."

"No, no, maybe, no more excuses. You better be there, you hear me?"

"Yeah."

"Man, if I don't see you there, I swear to God, don't make me come after you."

"Bring it on, bitch."

"Oh, so that's how it is going to be. If you want to see Mike Tyson, I will knock your ass out."

"Yeah, sure."

"I swear to God, you know what, scratch that, I will steal your car instead."

"What!?"

"I will steal your car."

"Why?"

"So, you can't go to work and have no excuse anymore."

"You are crazy, bro, so what am I supposed to do just sit around and drink with you?"

"Are you telling me that if someone is stealing your car, you will not have a drink, you will not drink your sorrow away? Come on, man."

"Well, yeah, in that case."

"Great, now I know how to make you come to my party. Whenever I throw one, I will steal your car the day before and return it afterwards."

"Bro, leave my car alone, fine. I will come to your stupid party even though this is blackmail."

"Call it whatever; I don't care. Your ass is mine now. Ha-Ha!"

"You blackmailing bastard, I hate you."

"I don't care if you hate me or not. I want to get you drunk, and then my revenge will be complete."

"Revenge!? What revenge, what did I do to you?"

"You refused my invitation; nobody refuses me, punk."

"Yeah, I was right. You are crazy and wonder why I don't show up at your parties," Alex says.

"Silence, peasant, the king has spoken."

"The king can kiss my ass."

"The king requests your presence on Saturday, 26th March. Be there or suffer the consequences."

"I think the Queen is in charge here."

"Well, I'm single. There is no Queen yet; that's why I have these parties. Maybe we can find a princess for you, my friend."

"I'm not your friend. I am Prince Alex, and you will address me accordingly," Alex says jokingly.

"Ha-Ha! Okay, your 'majesty', have you finished working today?"

"I'm heading back to central London to see if I can get one more trip, and then I will head home. You?"

"Still fishing at the airport, hoping to catch a "whale" and go home afterwards."

"Okay, then let me log into the app. See you next time."

"Take care, man, drive safe."

After a few minutes, Alex receives a trip request from Sushi Samba, which is near the Liverpool train station. When he arrives, he sees two men standing outside, one wearing a leather jacket and jeans and the other a tracksuit. Alex rolls down his window.

"Hey, is one of you Mike?"

"What?" The guy with the leather jacket approaches the car.

"Are you Mike? I'm your Uber driver."

"Yes."

The stranger turns to his friend and tells him something in a foreign language.

"Hop in."

Alex signals him to get inside the car. Mike jumps in front next to Alex as his friend gets in the back seat.

"So how are you, fellas, tonight, good?"

Alex drives away. The two men ignored his question.

"Euston Station, you take us there," Mike says, turning towards Alex.

"Sorry, but on the app, it shows me something else. Can you please change the destination?"

"Euston Station. Go, now."

"No, that's what I'm trying to explain to you. You need to change the destination. Take out your phone, and I will show you, okay?"

All of a sudden, the rider cancels the trip.

"Did you cancel the trip?" Alex asks as he checks the apps. Then, he looks back at his passengers and notices that none of them have their phones out.

"Your name is Mike, right?"

Alex turns towards the guy sitting next to him.

"What?"

"I'm Alex, what's your name?"

"Igor."

"Fuck, I picked up the wrong guy," Alex whispers to himself.

"Listen, fellas, I have to drop you off. I can't take you, okay? I'm sorry."

"No, you go to Euston," Igor says authoritatively.

"Listen, I can't. You have to request a trip. Do you have the Uber app?"

"Go, drive, Euston Station."

"I'm sorry, I can't take you if you don't have the app. I have to drop you off."

"No, no, you go to Euston."

Igor places his hand on Alex's shoulder. At this moment, Alex notices that his passengers are intoxicated.

"How am I going to get out of this without getting punched in the face? If I carry on talking with them, they might attack me while driving and probably crash the car because of them. Even if I pull over suddenly and then try to get them out, I might avoid getting hurt, but they may still damage my car. Either way, I'm fucked. What should I do? Should I take them to Euston Station? That would mean breaking the law, as I can only take passengers through the app." Alex thought deeply.

Alex carries on driving while trying to come up with a strategy, and then he sees a police car parked on the side of the road. The blue lights are on as two police officers are questioning a few pedestrians.

"Alex, you lucky bastard."

Alex pulls over and stops right behind the police car.

"Sorry, fellas, but I have to drop you off. I can't take you to Euston Station."

"No, don't stop here." Igor slams his fist on the dashboard.

"Sorry, fellas, this is as far as I can take you."

"No, no, go to Euston now!"

"Fellas, please get out. If not, you can talk to the police."Alex points out the police officers on the pavement. The two passengers get out and slam the doors behind them while grunting something in a foreign language back to Alex.

"That was close. Time to go home."

Alex drives back home from central London. As he reaches the A13 east towards Barking, his eyes become increasingly heavy. He is driving home while listening to the radio. Driving in the middle lane, he falls asleep for a few seconds while listening to the song "Guilty Conscience" by Eminem and Dr Dre. Chorus: "These voices, these voices I hear them, and when they talk, I'll follow, I'll follow, I'll follow."

His car slowly moves from the middle to the left lane, getting closer to the concrete wall on the side of the motorway.

Bang!

His left mirror is blown away as the car hits the concrete wall. Alex wakes up and panics, gripping the wheel and tries to regain control of the car.

"Fuck!"

Alex turns the wheel right, getting the car back on the road.

"Fuck me! I almost died. Two seconds more, and I would have been gone. I can't believe I blacked out like that. I was tired before, but I never imagined that I could fall asleep just like that. That's it, no more, no more long hours, no more hard work, time to take it easy. Fuck this shit, it is not worth it."

Sitting on the leather chair in front of Doctor Kingsley, Alex leans over and takes a sip of tea, being extra careful not to spill it.

"So, Alex, how have you been?" Doctor Kingsley asks.

"Good, good. I didn't spill the tea this time."

Alex smiles.

"I've noticed that."

Doctor Kingsley smiles back at Alex.

"The thing about anxiety is that once you become more aware, it becomes easier to counter it. By identifying the triggers and the moments when your anxiety levels are rising, you can make a conscious effort to suppress it or control it."

"Yeah, I have seen that. I feel more in control now."

"The whole purpose of our sessions is to help you get your power back. How is work?"

"Good."

"Okay, how about your social life?"

"Good, more or less?"

"Have you been socializing lately? Have you been out with your friend?"

"No, not really. He keeps inviting me to his parties, and I have been dodging it so far. But I sort of agree to go to his next party."

"And? Will you attend?"

"Well, I said yes, but I'm not sure."

"Why not?"

"I am very anxious about going."

"Why, what's your biggest fear about it?"

"That I will embarrass myself somehow."

"How exactly? What's the scenario that you see in

your mind?"

"I don't know, I will spill something, being clumsy again."

"And?"

"And people will make fun of me. When I'm nervous, my hands shake a bit, and people make fun of me."

"Did something like this happen before?"

"Yes, and people made fun of me. They implied that I'm afraid that I'm a coward. I'm not a coward; I can stand up for myself and know how to fight."

"Did you start a fight? Did you fight them?"

"No, not them. I fought against my bullies in the 10th grade, so I'm not a coward."

Doctor Kingsley adds an entry in his notebook.

"Care to share? Do you want to tell me what exactly happened when you were in school?"

"It's not much to say. There were these three boys that I saw every day on my way to school, and they bullied me."

"And?"

"And every day they were saying mean things to me, and eventually I fought them, I fought one of them."

"What were they saying to you?"

"I can't remember specifically what they were saying."

"How did the fight start? Do they attack you?"

"No, not exactly. One day, I saw only one of them. He said something mean as he passed by me. So, I slapped him in the face."

"That's how the fight started?"

"No, he ran away and threatened to get me back at

me the next day with his friends."

"What happened the next day?"

"There were only two of them instead of the usual three: the one that I slapped and one of his friends. But I was prepared to fight all three of them. If that doesn't make me brave, then I don't know what."

"When you say prepared, do you mean mentally?"

"Mentally and physically, I had this long key chain wrapped around my right fist. And I kept my hand in my pocket so they wouldn't see it."

"And then what happened?"

"Well, as soon as they saw me, they started talking trash."

"What did you say?" Doctor Kingsley asks.

"Nothing. I kept walking towards them. And when I was face to face with them, I started punching the one close to me. The other one ran away again."

"Then, what happened?"

"Well, the guy was completely off guard. I won the fight and walked away."

"Did you ever meet them afterwards?"

"Yeah, I still saw them every day, all three of them. But they didn't say anything to me ever again. They looked the other way every time we crossed paths."

"Is this the reason you avoid going to a party? Do you think you will be in a fight again?"

"No, I'm not some wild animal. I won't start a fight. It is just the thought of being embarrassed and humiliated in public."

"Have you ever told anyone about your anxiety?"

"No," Alex replies.

"Why not?"

"Because I'm not weak."

"Anxiety is not a weakness. And why is it so important to you to be perceived as strong?"

"Because I'm a man, and a man doesn't talk about his feelings. A man is supposed to be strong, and that's how I was raised anyway." Alex crosses his hands together over his chest.

"Is that how your parents raised you, to suppress your emotions?"

"Well, yeah, in some ways, I guess."

"How was your relationship with your father?"

"Normal, I guess."

"Did he interact with you? Did you play together?"

"Not much; he was working most of the time."

"What did he do for work?"

"He was in the military."

"What about your mother? How was your relationship with her?"

"She died when I was around five years old."

"How did that make you feel?"

"Sad, I guess," Alex replies sadly.

"What's your earliest childhood memory?"

"When she died."

"Care to share? What do you remember about her?"

"Not much to say, really."

"How did she die?"

"She had cancer, something internal, I found out later. They said that she was in terrible pain. She used to scream at night."

"Do you remember her screaming?"

"No, I remember being at our grandparents' house and waking up late at night."

"Why? Did something wake you up?"

"My grandmother was crying next to our bed."
"Our bed, you mean you and your brother."
"No, my Mom and I were sleeping in the same bed."
"Then what happened?"
"Well, I looked up, and my grandmother was crying, like I said, praying in a candlelight."
"And your mother?" Doctor Kingsley asks.
"She was sleeping peacefully; at least, that's what I thought. I didn't realize that she passed away. And she was sort of watching over me."
"What happened after that?"
"I went back to sleep eventually. And then, the next day, I realized what happened."
"Do you remember the funeral?"
"Not really, not much. I remember my dad yelling at me."
"Why?"
"I did something wrong, but I am not sure what."
"But he was mad at you?"
"Yeah."

Doctor Kingsley takes a moment to write some notes in his journal and then pauses for a moment. Alex breaks the silence.

"Do you think this is the cause of my anxiety? My mom died, and my dad yelling at me."
"Losing a parent can be a very traumatic experience that can have long-term implications over someone's mental health," explains Doctor Kingsley.
"Great, so I'm damaged goods."
"Everyone has been carrying emotional baggage from childhood—even me, with all my fancy degrees up there on the wall. One of the hardest

things in life for most people is to accept that some things are beyond our control. What happened in the past is not your fault, Alex."

"No, but I do have to suffer the consequences of that."

"You don't have to; you can learn to accept and then let go. Eventually, move on."

"So how do I do that?"

"You can start by going to your friend's party."

"Not sure that's a good idea."

"Don't be afraid to ask for help. You can confide in your friend and ask for support."

"Maybe, I don't know."

"If he is your friend like you said, he will be more than willing to help you."

"I guess," Alex says.

"Let me ask you this, why do you think he insists that you attend his party?"

"I guess because he wants to see me and spend some time together."

"Do you think that he wants to bully you or humiliate you?"

"No, I mean, we tease each other over the phone, but I don't think he will do anything like that."

"Do you think that if someone were to bully you by chance, he would just stand there and not come to your help and that he would not defend you?"

"No, I don't think he will just stand there and do nothing."

"Sounds like a good friend to me, who is trying to preserve your friendship. Perhaps you should reciprocate."

"Yeah, maybe you are right. I will think about it."

"You don't seem too sure about that."
"Yeah, it's not that. It's something else."
"Care to share it with me?"
"I was just wondering."
"About what?" asks Doctor Kingsley.
"Well, if I've suffered from anxiety for so many years, will it take the same number of years to get rid of it?"
"Anxiety is an emotion just like love, fear, or hate. The key is not to feel anything but to learn to control your emotions instead of your emotions controlling you."
"So, how long does it usually take to learn that?"
"It's hard to say, but it varies from person to person."
"I see."
"Learn to enjoy the journey. It may not feel like it, but we are making progress, which is more important. Lao Tzu said, "A journey of a thousand miles begins with a single step."
"Well, yeah, because they didn't have cars back then. Ha-ha," Alex laughs.
Doctor Kingsley smiles.
"That's true, but they did have horses."
"Yeah, right, so why he didn't take a horse? There are faster ways to get to your destination."
"I suppose sometimes, but there are no shortcuts when it comes to therapy."
"Well, I did a bit of research online."
"And what did you find?"
"I've read about hypnosis or self-hypnosis; you can reprogramme your mind, and that can speed up my recovery, no?"

"It varies; there are some factors that need to be taken under consideration, and it could have some side effects."

"Have you ever done it? Have you ever put someone under hypnosis?" Alex asks.

"A few times, yes. But we usually resort to hypnosis when dealing with some extreme traumas like child abuse, domestic violence, or rape."

"I see. I was really looking forward to this. I was reading that, basically, you can reprogram your brain just like that. " Alex snaps his fingers.

"It's a little more complicated than that."

"So, how does it work? How do you put someone under hypnosis?"

"The patient lies down and closes his eyes. I use that mechanical clock on my desk and tell them to relax and focus on the sound of the clock. Then, I started counting from ten to one. With each number decreasing, the patient goes into a more relaxed and deeper state. If done correctly, the patient should be under hypnosis when counting to one," Doctor Kingsley explains.

"Maybe I should try it at home, self-hypnosis."

"I would advise against that."

"Why not? Why take it slow when there is a faster way?"

"You are really set on this, are you? I tell you what, let's carry on with the current treatment with the medication that I prescribed you and our weekly sessions. And then, based on the outcome of this treatment, we can consider other forms of therapy."

"Yeah, I guess."

"In the meantime, promise me you will not try self-hypnosis."

"Yeah, okay."

"Alex, your well-being is my top priority, but I need you to cooperate. I mean it; self-hypnosis is not a joke. This could be very dangerous."

"Okay, okay, I promise."

◆ ◆ ◆

Alex, wearing a black suit and tie with a white shirt, looks in the living room mirror. He gets a phone call from his friend Dan.

"Hi, Dan."

"Hey, man, you had better be on your way."

"Yeah, I am waiting for a parcel to arrive, and I will be on my way."

"It sounds like you are making up excuses again."

"No, I swear it should be here in about half an hour, and I will be on my way soon."

"You better hurry up and then get dressed."

"I'm ready, bro. As soon as I get my parcel, I'm out

the door."

"Okay, better not lie to me."

"I'm not lying, bro. I am coming tonight, I swear."

"Okay, cool, ring me when you are here."

"Okay," Alex say as he ends the call.

Alex takes a seat on his sofa while browsing on his phone.

"Come on, Amazon, hurry up."

He gets up and opens the refrigerator.

"There is no alcohol in this house. I could use a drink right now."

Alex takes a seat back on his sofa. His right leg begins twitching again.

"What was that phrase, "Whatever happens, I can handle it."

He closes his eyes and repeats the phrase over and over again.

"Whatever happens, I can handle it. Whatever happens, I can handle it…"

Alex is startled by his doorbell and opens his eyes.

"Finally," he says.

He gets up and answers the door. When he opens the door, he sees his parcel down on the floor, and the delivery driver is already running down the stairs.

"Thank you!"

Alex shouts back at the delivery driver.

"What if I wasn't home, jackass. Great customer service; you get minus five stars today."

Alex sits back on his sofa and opens the parcel, revealing a mechanical nightstand clock. He places the clock down on his coffee table.

"Well, I hope you will do the trick. Shall we give it a go?"

Dan is calling him again on the phone.

"Oh, for fuck sakes! What? "

Alex answers the phone.

"Are you coming, man? What are you doing?"

"I'm coming now; I am literally out the door, okay?"

"Hurry up, man."

"Stop stressing me like I'm late for work or something, for fuck sake."

"Alright, alright, calm down. How long does it take you to get here?"

"Half an hour."

"Okay, move it then."

"Bro, I'm on the way. Stop calling me."

Alex hangs up the phone.

◆ ◆ ◆

A white Toyota Prius stops in front of a flat building on Romford Road in Stratford, London. It's an old grey building with a small, enclosed parking area in front. To access the building, you must pass through a black metal gate. Alex tries to open the gate, but it is locked. He calls Dan over the phone.

"Hi, bro, I'm outside."

"What? Where are you?"

"I'm outside."

"What?"

"I'm outside. Tell me the access code."

"The code is 5, 3…"

"What I can't hear, bro."

"I said the code is 5, 3…"

"Bro, I can't hear you; just text me the code."

Alex hangs up, and then he receives a text message with the code. He opens the gate and walks inside the building. He can already hear the music as he goes up the stairs to the fourth floor, and the music gets louder. He knocks on Dan's door, but nobody answers. He calls Dan again.

"Hey bro, open the door."

"What?"

"I said, open the door. I'm outside your flat."

"What?"

"Open the fucking door, bro!"

Dan opens the door. He is a tall, well-built man with short blonde hair, blue eyes, a small scar above his right eye, and a Viking beard. Dan is dressed casually in a pair of blue jeans and a white polo t-shirt.

"What?"

"You jackass."

"I'm sorry. Do I know you?"

"Very funny."

"Look at you, all dressed up like James Bond. Come here." Dan gives Alex a "bear hug," suffocating him.

"Well, you said we are going to some clubs later."

"Fuck yeah, we are going, we are getting wasted tonight."

"Not so sure about that."

"No, no, you don't have a say about that. It's not optional. Now get your ass inside, let's get drunk."

Dan guides Alex into the kitchen, passing through the living room packed with people sitting on the sofa on the left side and at the table on the right. A few people standing up. Everyone enjoys themselves, drinks, smokes, engages in different conversations, and forms small groups.

"Hey everyone, say hello to my friend Alex," Dan shouts at them.

"Hey, how are you?"

"Hi!"

Some people respond, some acknowledge Alex with a nod, and some are completely oblivious.

"Hi," Alex greets them with a soft voice—the loud music covers his greeting.

Dan signals to Alex to follow him into the kitchen area.

"Hey, what do you want to drink?"

"I don't know."

"I got everything: beer, whiskey, vodka, you name it."

"I think I will start with a beer, thanks."

"Ah, man, don't go soft on me."

"No worries, the night it's still young."

"Fuck that, how about a jack and coke."

"Okay, I guess."

"Damn right."

Dan prepares the drinks while Alex takes a better look around.

"I didn't realize you know so many people."

"Oh, and this is only half of them. There is still more to come, and that's why I suggested going to a club."

"Wow, you really are popular," says Alex.
"What can I say? I'm the man," Dan replied.
"Do you want ice in yours?"
"Yeah, sure, thanks."
"Here you go, mate."
"Oh, are we English now?"
"Of course, mate, it's about bloody time. I've been living here for 7 years now."
"Can you turn the music down? I don't want to go deaf."
"Do you think this is loud? Wait until we get to the club."
"Fuck me," Alex says loudly.
"Fine, then let's go on the balcony. I was playing poker with some friends."
"I'm not much of a poker player, to be honest."
"Relax; we don't play for money; we just want to pass the time until the rest show up."

Dan and Alex go outside on the balcony, where there is a small round table and four chairs, and two men are playing poker.

"These are my friends, Jhon and Steve."

Jhon is 30 years old, with a fit body, blond hair, and blue eyes; he wears a black t-shirt, blue jeans, white trainers, and a gold chain on his neck. He also has some tattoos on his arms. Steve is the same age, overweight, with dark hair and brown eyes. Wears a long blue-sleeved shirt with black jeans and brown shoes.

"Hi, fellas."

Alex reaches out for a handshake.

"Look at you, lad. Are you trying to be James Bond or something?"

Jhon extends his arms to Alex.

"That's what I said."
Dan taps Steve on the shoulder. "Hey, move over, make some room."
"Where do you want me to go? There is no more space here," Steve replied angrily.
"Just squeeze that beer belly of yours," Dan says.
"If you want to squeeze something, here is something you can squeeze."
Steve point at this penis.
"I will do it if that gets you to move your fat ass."
"That's illegal, you know."
Jhon lights up a cigarette.
"What, squeezing someone's dick." Steve smiles.
Jhon slams the lighter on the table.
"No grabbing a child's pennis."
Everyone burst into laughter apart from Steve.
"Fuck you guys."
Steve moves over.
"Okay, everyone, settle down. Let's play already."
Jhon snaps his fingers.
"Okay, okay."
Steve deals the cards.
"You have two left hands, mate."
Jhon puts his cards face down on the table.
"I'm happy with what I see."
Dan lights a cigarette.
"So, who else is coming?"
Steve opens a beer.
"Some girls are late as usual."
Dan exhales some smoke.
"Is that one coming? What's her name, the brunette with blue eyes?"
"Who, Christine?"

"Yeah, that's the one. I got my eyes on her, on her banging ass, to be precise."

"Hands off, she is reserved for my boy here."

Dan points at Alex.

"Nah, mate, if she is single, then I'm putting my chips down."

"Take your chips back. She is off-limits."

"It's okay, but I'm also putting my chips down."

Alex throws some chips in the pot.

"I like you, mate. I raised you ten."

Jhon throws some chips.

"I'm out."

Dan throws his cards away.

"Me too."

Steve pulls back on his chair.

"I see your ten and raise you twenty."

Alex adds more chips to the pot.

"It looks like it's just you and me, mate. Let's end this quickly, shall we? I'm all in." Jhon says, putting all his chips into the pot.

"Someone is in a rush to lose."

Dan blows some smoke.

"I never lose, mate."

Jhon snaps his fingers. Alex takes a deep breath.

"What's the matter, mate? Lose your courage?"

Jhon looks Alex dead in the eyes.

"No, I am just taking my time to savour my victory. I'm all in."

"Okay, now let's see them."

Dan throws his cigarette bud over the balcony.

"Ladies first."

Jhon snaps his fingers.

"No, you first mate."

Alex snaps his fingers at Jhon.

"Oh, come on, fellas."

Steve chugs his bear down.

"Come on, Alex, be the bigger man."

Dan places his hand on Alex's shoulder.

"Fine."

Alex reveals his cards and says he has a full house.

"Not bad, mate. But like I said, I never lose."

Jhon reveals a royal flush and wins.

"Damn, I was too sure of myself."

"Live and learn; I am always the champion. Now you know."

Jhon snaps his fingers with a big smile on his face. Alex looks down at his shoes, disappointed. Dan receives a phone call.

"Hello, yeah, what do you mean you can't find it? You have been here before, alright? I'm coming down."

Dan hangs up the phone.

"Was that Christine?"

Jhon leans forward.

"No, it was someone else. Alex, come with me, man."

Dan and Alex leave the flat. As they walk down the stairs, Dan turns back at Alex.

"It was Christine."

Dan winks at Alex.

"Oh, you snake."

"What? I'm looking after my boy."

"Thanks, bro. I owe you."

"Of course you do. You shall name your first-born child Dan."

"What if it's a girl?"

"Then Diana."

Alex and Dan walk towards the gate and see a group of people waiting. Dan places his hand on Alex's shoulder.

"Hey, you see that girl there on the right."

"The one with the black dress, yeah, she is hot."

"That's Christine."

"Wow!" Alex exclaims.

"Don't mess it up."

Dan opens the gate.

"Hello, hello, come on in people. This is my friend Alex."

Alex nods his head.

"Hey, Christine, this is the guy I was talking to you about."

"Hi, Alex, nice to meet you."

"Hi, um, nice to meet you too, Christine."

Dan hugs them both.

"Look at you; you look nice and classy. Am I a matchmaker or what?"

Dan takes the lead as they go inside.

"Alright, people, tonight we are getting drunk, and I mean everyone, no exceptions."

Everyone got cheering.

"Wow!?"

"Yeah!?"

Dan guides everyone inside his flat. Alex and Christine make their way into the kitchen. Alex touches Christine on her shoulder.

"Um, so can I get you a drink?"

"Sure, what have you got there?"

"Whiskey, vodka-"

"Wow, are you trying to get me drunk?"

"No, I'm-"

"I'm joking, and you need to relax a bit."
"Yeah, maybe."
"Do you have anything lighter?"
"I think there is beer."
"That's better."

Alex opens the refrigerator door.

"There is Budweiser and Corona."
"Corona, please, thanks."

Alex grabs a bottle, but when he turns around to hand it to Christine, he accidentally drops it. The bottle smashes and breaks into pieces on the floor.

"Fuck!" Alex says disappointedly.
"It's okay. I will help you clean."
"No, no, it is fine. I will do it."

Alex gives Christine another bottle.

"Here you go."
"Thanks. Are you sure you don't need any help?"
"Yeah, it's fine, no worries."

Alex takes some kitchen tissues, gets down on one knee, and starts cleaning the floor. Jhon comes over and joins them.

"Hey Christine, I see you are always making men fall on their knees for you."

Christine smiles while playing with her hair.

"Hey Jhon, how are you?"
"I'm good now that I see you."
"Oh, stop it."

Jhon looks down at Alex.

"Mate, what the hell are you doing down there? Are you trying to look upskirt on Christine, you naughty boy."

Alex ignores John's remark. While Christine grabs John's arm.

"Hey, don't be rude."

"I'm not. I'm just looking after you, my love. Hey Alex, mate, could you pass a beer since you are already down there?"

Jhon winks at Christine. Alex give Jhon a beer.

"Cheers, love."

Jhon opens his beer and smiles at Christine. Dan turns off the music.

"Okay, people, listen up. We are going to the club now to get our groove on. After that, we will come back here. You all know if you party with me, you party all night long, baby. Let's go, everyone, out and get a couple of Ubers."

Everyone cheers.

"Wow!"

"Yeah!?"

Dan, Alex, and everyone from the party are waiting outside in front of the building for the Ubers to arrive. They are talking loudly, shouting, and screaming; some are smoking, and others are sipping beer. A few neighbours poke their heads out the windows, disturbed by the noise. As the Uber cars start coming one by one, their group gets smaller. Dan, Alex, and Jhon are among the last to leave. As the car stops, Alex rushes to open the door for Christine.

"Such a gentleman, thanks."

Alex is about to get in the car when Jhon sneaks in before him.

"Cheers, mate."

"Hey!"

Christine tries to push Jhon out of the car.

"It's okay, love; he will grab the next one."

Jhon slams the door, leaving Alex behind alone on the

pavement as everyone else leaves.

"I hate that guy."

Alex sobs for a moment, then takes out his phone and orders an Uber for himself. Outside of the Club, Dan checks to see if everyone made it.

"Okay, everyone seems to be here; no, my boy, Alex, is not here."

"He got lost in the woods." Jhon laughs.

"You left him behind."

Christine gives Jhon a mean look.

"Is nature love, the weak are left behind-"

"Okay, everyone, go in. I will stay and wait for Alex."

A few minutes go by, and Alex arrives. Dan opens the car door.

"Hey man, where have you been?"

"I had to get another car since I was left behind. Thank you very much."

"What, what did I do?"

"Nothing, let's get inside."

"Man, what are you doing with Christine?"

"What do you mean?"

"Every time I turn around, she is with Jhon."

"Well, he stole my Uber."

"What about back home in the kitchen? She was with him; where the hell were you?"

"Well, I was there."

"I didn't see you."

"That's because I was on the floor."

"What the hell were you doing on the floor?"

"It's, it doesn't matter."

"Man, get it together, or he will steal, not just your Uber."

Dan and Alex make their way inside. The club is packed to the brim with people everywhere. Music is playing very loud, and there is a show of lights changing their directions and colours on the beats of the music. They slowly navigate through the scene of people all the way to the bar and join their group. Dan orders two beers and passes one to Alex; after that, he grabs Christine's hand and nods to Alex.

"Let's dance people."

The entire group moves to the dance floor. Everyone is dancing and having a good time. Alex and Christine dance in the vicinity of each other, exchanging looks from time to time. Jhon "accidentally" bumps into Alex, making Alex spill his beer all over Christine's dress.

"I'm so sorry."

Alex apologises to Christine.

"Hey, be more careful, mate."

Jhon soft punches Alex in the chest.

"You be more careful."

"What's that supposed to mean?"

"You pushed me."

"I was dancing, mate; you were the one who tripped. If you don't know how to dance, get off the floor."

Dan intervenes between Alex and Jhon to calm the situation.

"Hey, hey, you two, break it off. Christine, I'm sorry, but it's only beer. It will wash off, or you can use the hand drier from the toilet and dry it."

Christine goes to the toilet with one of her friends. Dan pulls Alex to the side.

"What are you doing, man?"

"It wasn't me, I swear, it's that jackass."

"Man, you need to relax or maybe focus. Come with me."

Alex and Dan go to the toilet. Dan enters one of the stalls.

"Come here, man."

Dan holds the door open for Alex.

"No thanks, bro. I'm not standing by you while you take a shit."

"I'm not doing that. Just get in here, will you?"

Alex follows him inside. Dan closes the door and pulls a small plastic bag out of his pocket with white dust inside.

"Is that what I think it is?"

Alex pulls back.

"Yes, this magic dust will help you solve all your problems."

"No, bro, I'm not doing drugs."

"Yeah, you will."

"No, I'm not."

"Just one line, maybe two," Dan tried to convince Alex.

"Bro, I don't know."

"Man, listen to me; just take a chance once in a while; that's all I'm asking. I promise it won't kill you, okay?"

"One line, maybe."

"How about two? It looks like you need some extra courage tonight."

After doing cocaine in the toilet, Dan and Alex come back out on the dance floor only to see Christine and Jhon kissing. Dan turns toward Alex.

"I'm sorry, man. But hey, we are in a club. Let's find you another girl."

"Yeah, maybe. Let me grab another beer. Do you

want one?"

"No, I'm good. I will see you on the dance floor, okay?"

Dan joins their group while Alex sobs and watches them from afar, lost in his own thoughts. Alex goes to the bar and chugs down a beer in a few seconds. After that, he takes one last look at Jhon and Christine while they slowly dance and then sneaks out of the club. Alex wanders around the cold streets of London, making his way to the Victoria Embankment, where he sits on a bench waiting for the sunrise. When Alex arrives at his building is full daylight outside. A blue butterfly flying over some flowers catches his attention. He stops and gazes for a while. The butterfly makes a turn and flies towards Alex; the butterfly circles Alex a few times and then flies away into the sky. Alex then makes his way into his flat and launches himself on the sofa, lost in his mind. Turning his head around, he sees the mechanical clock he ordered the day before.

"Ah, yes, should we give this a try then?"

Alex lays down on his back in a comfortable position and starts a countdown.

"Okay, ten, nine, eight, seven, six, five, four, three, two, one..."

◆ ◆ ◆

ROYAL FLUSH

Late at night, Alex, dressed in a black suit and tie, is waiting in a white Mercedes-Benz AMG outside The Savoy in London. The hotel is located on the Strand. It has a narrow street connecting the hotel to the main road, the Strand, creating a small junction with a traffic light. In front of the hotel, there is a small water fountain that serves as a roundabout for cars coming in and out of the hotel. Above the entrance, we can see the name of the hotel with blue neon lights and a couple of flags waving in the wind above the hotel logo. In the middle of the flags stands the golden statue of Peter of Savoy, like a Greek God on Mount Olympus. Alex takes a moment to admire the luxurious interior of the car, the brown leather interior, checking the dashboard and the navigation system.

"I can get used to this."

A man wearing a business suit knocks on his window.

"Are you my Uber, Alex?"

"Yes, sir. Let me help you with your luggage."

Alex presses the button to open the booth and then steps outside of his vehicle.

"No worries, sir, I will get those for you. Why don't

you get inside and make yourself comfortable?"

Alex opens the back door for his passenger and then places the luggage inside the booth. After that, Alex gets back into the driver's seat.

"Ok, let's see where we are heading."

"Heathrow Terminal 1, please."

"Sure thing, sir."

"If you get me there fast, there is a big tip for you."

"Hmm, I will do my best."

"Come on, Alex, show me what you have got; I will give you £100."

"Ok, but it's not going to be a smooth ride."

"Fine by me, hit it."

"Okay, just give me a moment. Someone who drives fast; I know the guy from the Transporter movies."

Alex stares at a fixed point on his dashboard and starts counting from ten to one. His passenger watches him with a surprised look on his face, trying to figure out what is happening. After finishing the countdown, Alex looks back at his passengers with a serious expression on his face, giving a different vibe than a moment ago. Even his tone of voice changed.

"Put your seat belt on."

"Oh, come on, Alex, buddy, just drive already."

"Not until you put your seatbelt on."

"Jesus, you are taking all the fun out."

"Safety first, rule number one."

"Okay, okay, here the seatbelt is on now drive."

"Not yet."

"What now?"

"Waiting for the light to turn green."

"Can you at least drive up closer to the traffic

light?"

"Don't disrupt the driver rule number 2."

"So many rules in the UK, can't wait to go back to the land of the free home of-"

Alex takes off mid-sentence as the light turns green. He makes a hard left turn on the Strand, passing at full speed by Charing Cross station. Reaching Trafalgar Square roundabout, he takes the third exit to The Mall. This is the main artery road that leads straight to Buckingham Palace. When they reach Queen Victoria Memorial in front of Buckingham Palace, Alex makes a hard right turn on Constitution Hill.

"Jesus." His passenger grabs the door handle with both hands.

Constitution Hill leads to Wellington Arch in Hyde Park Corner, where Alex takes the second exit on Knightsbridge Road. And makes a left turn on Brompton Road, passing Knightsbridge underground station. Keeps driving straight ahead, passing London Oratory Catholic Church down Cromwell Road towards West Kensington. This road merges with A4, passing through Hammersmith Flyover and then Chiswick, leading to the M4 motorway. Reaching the M4, Alex pushes the car to the limits, driving at full speed and taking every car in sight. His passenger starts to feel sick as Alex constantly changes lanes, and then he takes the first exit to Heathrow Terminal 1, making an abrupt stop in the drop-off area.

"We are here, Sir."

"Jesus, you are something else."

"I believe you owe me £100."

"£100, yeah, right, you are lucky if I don't report you."

"Rule number 5: any changes, adjustments, or deviations from the original contract are not acceptable."

"Fine, here." The passenger hands over to Alex two £50 bills.

"Now, come on and help me with the bags."

"Rule number 7: if the package includes a passenger, the passenger is responsible for loading and unloading."

"Jesus, you really are crazy."

The passenger gets out and slams the door behind him. Alex puts the money in his wallet and grabs the steering wheel.

"Okay, to the next contract... wait, what contract? Stop! I have to reset—butterfly, butterfly."

Alex becomes his original self again.

"Wow, that was intense. I didn't know I could drive like that. This self-programming stuff really works. It's nice. Oh, shit, I forgot about the speed cameras. Nice going, Alex the Transporter. Now I'm going to get a ticket."

Alex drives back to London, slowly enjoying the sunrise while listening to the radio. When he reaches Hyde Park Corner, he receives a ride request from Piccadilly Circus.

"Okay, one more, and that's it."

When he approaches the Piccadilly Circus Junction, Alex sees two blonde girls standing right next to the traffic lights.

"Is that my trip? Why do people always wait in the middle of the junction, and where am I going to stop? Stupid people. Hmm, let's hope the lights don't change."

Alex stops at the traffic lights and rolls down his window.

"Hey, is one of you Aldona?"

"Yes, me, I'm Aldona, and this is my friend, Lina."

"I'm Alex, your Uber."

"Great."

"Hurry up, get in. I'm not supposed to stop here."

"Okay, Okay."

Aldona gets in the front seat next to Alex and Lina in the back seat.

"Nice car."

"Thanks, it's my dream car."

Aldona takes a sip from a bottle of Moet and then hands it to Alex.

"Here, have a taste."

"What! are you crazy? I'm driving."

"So what?"

"What do you mean so what?"

Lina leans forward.

"Come party with us."

"Yeah, don't be shy."

Aldona places her hand on Alex's leg.

"I'm not... shy; I have to focus on driving."

"So, you party with us at home?"

"Yeah, you go home with us, Wow!"

Lina leans back in her seat.

"Maybe, I don't know."

"Maybe yes."

Aldona slides her hand on Alex's genitals.

"Shit!"

Alex hits the brakes as he almost crashes into the car in front of him.

"Careful, Alex."

"Hey, can you stop distracting me?"
"What happened? What did you do, Aldona?"
Lina leans forward.
"Nothing."
Aldona removes her hand from Alex's genitals and leans back into her seat.
"I'm too sexy. Alex can't take his eyes off me."
"Oh, what about me, Alex? Do you think I'm sexy?"
Lina whispers into Alex's ear.
"I think you both are very sexy."
Alex blushes, and then Lina bites his ear slowly and sensually.
"Okay, okay."
Alex pulls away.
"You girls need to let me drive. Stop distracting me."
"Hey, go back there. You want to get us killed?"
Aldona pushes Lina back.
"I want to party. Wow! With Alex."
"I want to party with Alex first, and that's why I'm in front."
"Ladies, please."
"Ha, ha, Alex is blushing."
Aldona pinches Alex on the cheek.
"Hey, don't disturb the driver."
Alex pushes her hand away.
"So, where are you from, Alex?"
"Romania."
"Romania?! Romanian people drink, so why did you say no?"
"Because I'm driving."
"Yeah, you can have a sip, so what? Are you sure you are Romanian?"

"Yes, of course, I'm Romanian, give me the bottle." Alex snatches the bottle from Aldona's hands and chugs down a big sip.

"Yeah, now we can party like in Lithuania."

"You are from Lithuania both?"

Alex hands over the bottle of Moet back to Aldona.

"Yes, we are Lithuanian girls, right Lina?!"

Lina has fallen asleep in the back seat.

"Hey, wake up!"

Aldona turns back to Lina and shakes her leg.

"Wake up!"

"What! We are here?"

Lina wakes up.

"Yes, we are here in London. Where are you?"

"I don't know."

"Ha, ha, I think you need some "vitamin."

Aldona leans back into her seat.

"Yes! Do we have any left?"

"I think so. What about you, Alex, do you want some "vitamin"?"

"What? What vitamin?"

"You know, "white vitamin," energy."

"Oh, I don't know, maybe."

"To party with two girls, you need energy, Alex."

Lina leans forward.

"Yeah, so you can go all night long, baby."

"It's the day already, bitch," Aldona said.

"Fine, all day long, baby."

"Go slow, Alex. We are almost there."

"We are here, stop."

"Shut up bitch. It's next street on the left." Aldona pushes Lina back into her seat.

"Where are you taking us, Alex?" Lina looks out

the window.

"Home."

Alex glances in the rear-view mirror.

"Home?! Your home or our home?"

"Yours."

"No, my boyfriend is there, our boyfriends. Let me out." Lina clutches the door handle.

"Shut up bitch."

"Boyfriends?!"

Alex gives Aldona a very confused look.

"Hey, everyone, calm down."

"But you have boyfriends, so?"

"So, what?! We are waiting for them to go to work, but they should be leaving soon."

"I don't know."

"It's okay, relax."

"Shouldn't I park here then?"

"No, take the next left, and I will show you where to stop."

Alex turns left and starts looking for an empty parking space, as there are cars parked on both sides of the street.

"I see two empty spaces, one on the left and another on the right."

"Go to that one on the right."

"Are you sure? Where is your house?"

"Just go there, park there."

Aldona points to the parking space on the right down the street.

"I see it, but which one is your house?"

"It's fine; they will not see us. We just wait until they leave."

Alex parks the car.

"Where is the "vitamin"?"

Lina jumps up from her seat.

"Give me, give me!"

Aldona takes out from her purse a phone, a small plastic bag with cocaine in it, a credit card, and a five-pound note. She uses the card to draw a line of cocaine on her phone and rolls the "fiver" into the shape of a straw. Then she hands over the phone and the "straw" to Lina.

"Okay, you go first, then Alex, and then me."

Lina sniffs out the line without hesitation, out of the line in a split second, and then hands over the set back to Aldona.

"Okay, Alex, it's your turn."

Aldona prepares a line of cocaine for Alex and passes it to him.

"Um, which nostril should I use, the left or the right?"

"It doesn't matter whatever."

"The right one is always the right one."

Lina leans forward.

"It doesn't matter, stupid; they both go to the brain."

"No, because the right nostril goes to the right side of the brain; that's where you want it to go."

Lina points her finger to the left side of her head.

"You are pointing to the left side, stupid."

"No."

"Yes, you are."

"No, because he sees me in reverse."

"What?"

"I'm pointing to the left and he sees the right in the mirror."

"He is not looking into the mirror, stupid."

"Exactly."

"Alex, go already."

Aldona turns towards Alex and watches him take his line of cocaine, and then she prepares a line for herself. As Aldona is about to sniff her line, two men in their twenties dressed as construction workers come out from the house next to the car. Alex sees them and turns to Aldona.

"It's that your boyfriends?"

"Where?"

Lina peaks out the window. Aldona inhales her cocaine in a second and then looks up.

"Shit! Relax, they will not see us."

"What do you mean? They are looking right at us. Great, you made me park right in front of your house."

"Relax."

Aldona ducks down, hoping her boyfriend doesn't see her. One of the men comes over, knocks at the back window, and signals to Lina to get out. Then he pulls the handle to open the door, but it's locked. Lina tries to open the door, but she also fails. Then they start shouting at each other in Lithuania while both try to open the door simultaneously.

"Atidaryk duris! (Open the door)."

The man shouts at Lina through the car window.

"Laukti, laukti (wait, wait)."

Lina desperately tries to open the door.

"Atidaryk, atidaryk! (Open, open)"

The other man calls out Aldona to get out of the car.

"Aldona! Aldona!"

Aldona is also struggling to open the car door, while Alex is confused by the whole situation, turning his head back and forth.

"Sorry, sorry, my bad, I forgot to unlock the doors."

Alex presses a button on his side door and unlocks the car.

"Sorry, sorry, it's an automated system."

The girls get out of the car and get into a big argument on the pavement. From time to time, the men point at Alex.

"Great, there goes my chance. I don't like how this looks. I had better get the hell out of here before I end up having a Ménage à Trois with these guys."

Alex starts the car and drives away in a hurry.

◆ ◆ ◆

Late in the evening in London, at The Eagle Pub in Farringdon, two security agents dressed all in black guard the double door entrance. The pub is situated on the A201 Farringdon Road corner with Baker's Row. It has six large windows, three on the left side of the entrance and three on the right side. The large windows offer a clear view inside the pub, which is packed with people sitting at the bar or the tables, everyone with a drink in their hands and having a good time. The exterior of the pub is painted in a dark lime green colour with the name of the pub written on top of the entrance. And above it sits an eagle statue. Both security men are tall and muscular; one of them is scrolling through his phone while the other is glancing inside the pub through the window from time to time, and then he decides to break the silence.

"Yo, are you still banging Jim?"

"What?" While he puts his phone back into his pocket.

"Are you banging Jim?"

"Yeah, bruv."

"My G, how many times a week?"

"Three, four times, sometimes more. You?"

"Nah, I'm slacking off lately."

"Why?"

"I got this "peng thing," so I've been busy lately, you know."

"Where is she from?"

"Jamaica, I think."

"No, I mean the ends, G."

"Peckham."

"Are you going down to Peckham?"

"No, bruv, I ain't getting myself "wet" for no peng thing, you get me?"

"Say less. It's mental, so many stabbings. Nowadays, the youth have knives or something."

"Yeah, I know maybe we should have a Brexit for London, like north and south. Do you get me?"

"That's not a bad idea, even though I don't get it."

"Get what?"

"The Brexit, what's the point? We are not in Europe anyway, innit?"

"Of course we are."

"Nah, G, we are on Island innit, so technically, we aren't in Europe."

"Bruv, it is not about that. It's politics, you get me."

"Fam, we are not in Europe, and we have never been."

"What are you talking about, bruv? Of course, we are."

"So how come we still had the pound, you know? Everyone there uses euros."

"That's a good point, bruv. I don't know if they made a deal or something."

"And now they want to cancel it."

"Something like that. I think the old geezers voted for Brexit. They don't want people coming here anymore."

"Say less; that makes sense."

"What, you are taking their side?"

"Well, it makes sense, you know, that we are on an island."

"Yeah, so?"

"It's limited space, my G, were you gonna put all the people. The whole country is going to be packed like the Central Line Train."

"I don't know, build more flats, you get me."

"Facts, you should be the prime minister, my G."

"Bruv, if I were in charge, the whole country would be banging, you get me."

Alex, wearing a black suit and tie, walks slowly toward the pub with one hand in his pocket. One of the security agents notices him approaching the pub.

"Yo, it's time to be professional."

He signals to his coworkers that a potential customer is heading their way.

"Alright, say less."

Alex stops in front of them.

"Evening fellas."

"Good evening, sir; go ahead."

"Thanks."

Alex stands still in front of them.

"Don't worry about ID, just go."

"Thanks."

Alex is still not moving.

"You're all right?"

"Yeah."

"Are you sure?"

The two security agents exchange looks.

"Yeah, I'm fine…"

Alex pushes open the doors and walks in slowly. He then stops and looks around. The pub is full of businesspeople drinking, laughing, and having a good time. He notices a few single women by the bar. He takes one step forward, stops, turns around, and walks back out. The security agents turn their attention to Alex.

"Leaving already?"

"No, not really."

"What happened? Did you see your ex there?"

"No, I just need a moment."

Alex takes a deep breath and walks back inside.

"Yo, this guy is mental."

"This office job will kill you; you get me."

"Say less, all that stress and anxiety and shit."

Alex walks back out again.

"Are you sure you are all right?"

"Yeah."

Alex takes a few deep breaths.

"You should get a drink to calm down. Do you get me?"

"Or go home and chill."

"Yeah, maybe."

Alex takes a deep breath and walks back in. Two

seconds later, he is back out. He starts walking away, turning left on Baker's Row. One of the security agents says his goodbyes as Alex walks away.

"See you next time, Mr. Bond."

Alex stops and turns his head back.

"What?"

"You know Bond, James Bond, because of the suit you get me."

"Ah yeah…"

Alex continues walking up the street, then stops and rests with his back against a building.

"James Bond, huh? I wish I were…Wait a minute, I could be; why not?"

Alex fixes his gaze down at the pavement, focusing on one point.

"Okay, let's do this, James Bond, ten, nine, eight… one."

A few moments later, Alex returns to the pub, greeted by the same two security agents.

"Hey, look who's back?"

"Are you sure this time?"

"I'm positive I'm walking out of this pub with a gorgeous woman by my arm."

Alex smiles and walks inside extremely confident with his chest out and laser focus gaze. The two security agents stand there waiting for Alex to come back, rushing again.

"I bet you five quid he is coming back out again."

"Make it ten."

"Are you sure, bruv?"

"Yeah, there was something different about him this time. Did you get me?"

"It's your money, say less."

Inside the pub, there are three women by the bar. One of them catches Alex's eye. A beautiful brunette is wearing a tight skirt with high heels and a formal shirt with white and blue stripes. She notices him entering. They both make eye contact for a few seconds, and then she turns to her friends. Alex goes straight to the bar and sits near the beautiful brunette. She turns and gives Alex a look.

"Hey."

"Hi."

Alex winks at her and then turns to the bartender.

"I will have a Martini and an Aperol Spritz."

After that, Alex turns his whole body towards the beautiful brunette, looking intensely at her in the eyes as the bartender places the drinks on the counter. The brunette woman looks down at the drinks and then back at Alex.

"Who said you can buy me a drink?"

"Who said it's for you?"

Alex gives his credit card to the bartender while the brunette woman is shocked for a moment by Alex's answer, which is clearly not what she was expecting. Confused by the whole situation, all sorts of thoughts going through her brain. She desperately tries to recover from this embarrassing moment where she assumed the drink was for her.

"Well, I'm married anyway, so."

"Don't feel bad about it. We all make mistakes," says Alex as he winks at her.

"Happily married."

"Good for you."

"What about you? Are you married?"

"Nope."

Alex smiles.

"But I came close a few times."

"A few times, what does that mean?"

"It depends, I guess."

"Depends on what?"

"Does sleeping with married women count or not?"

"I don't think so."

"I didn't think so either, and that's why I said it a few times instead of using an actual number."

They both smile at each other.

"So, what's your name, or should I just call you "happily married?"

"I'm Cintya."

Cintya extends her arm for a handshake. Alex refuses to shake it; he just stands still.

"What's wrong? You don't shake hands with a woman?"

"Since this is not a business meeting, I will have to decline it. My two options are to kiss your hand or to kiss you. Which one should I choose..."

Alex gazes intensely into Cintya's eyes. Another woman comes along, sits between them, and cuts their sensual interaction.

"Sorry, guys, I just want to get myself another drink. Can I have an Aperol Spritz?"

"You can have this one; it hasn't been touched."

"You are quite the gentleman, thank you."

Alex hands her the drink.

"Who is your friend here, Cintya?"

"I don't know; he didn't introduce himself."

"How rude of me, I'm Alex."

"Hi Alex, I'm Kristy."
Kristy extends her arm to Alex, and they shake hands.
"Nice to meet you, Alex."
"Likewise."
"Come and join us at our table."
"You know what? I could also go for another drink."
Cintya cuts in.
"Alex, do you mind being a gentleman again?"
"Not at all, my pleasure."
"Kristy, why don't you go back to the table? Alex and I will join you shortly."
"Okay, okay, I wouldn't want to interrupt your little date here."
"It's not a date."
Cintya pulls back.
"I agree. I wouldn't take anyone on a date in a pub."
Kristy walks away, and Alex orders another drink.
"One Aperol Spritz."
"So, what's your ideal date then?"
Cintya moves closer to Alex, closing the gap between them.
"It depends."
"On what?"
"On how flexible you are."
Alex smiles at her. Cintya looks down for a moment and then back at Alex, smiling.
"You are good, I give you that."
"Wait until you get to know me."
Alex winks at her.
"I'm actually bad, very bad."
Alex grabs her by the waist and pulls her closer to him.

He looks her intently in the eyes, then smiles and goes in for a kiss. Cintya kisses him back, completely lost in the moment she surrenders to him. Alex stops and breaks from her embrace.

"Okay, now that we have that out of the way, shall we join your friends?"

"Your drink, sir."

"Perfect timing, my good man."

Alex and Cintya make their way to her friends, navigating slowly through the sea of people. Cintya introduces him.

"Hey, everyone, this is Alex."

"Hi."

"Hi."

"Nice to meet you, Alex."

"So, Alex, what do you do?"

Kristy moves in closer to Alex.

"I do... Whatever it takes to get the job done."

"Oh, we have a mysterious man here tonight, ladies."

"And what that job might be?"

"He does married women, apparently."

Cintya jumps in on the conversation.

"I'm married, do me."

Kristy smiles at Alex, and the rest of the group starts laughing.

"Well, I only do happily married women."

"I'm happy once or twice a week."

Kristy grabs Alex's right arm, in which he holds his Martini glass.

"I suppose that counts."

"Here's to happily married. Cheers, everyone!"

Cintya raises her glass and encourages everyone to

do the same. Kristy is forced to let go of Alex's arm.
"Cheers!"
"Cheers!"
"In that case, Cintya is miserable because her husband is away for the week."
"That's a shame."
"Why? Did you want to meet him?"
"No, not really, but sex is more intense on the risk of getting caught."
"So, you are the "only live once" type of guy?"
"No, that's not true. You only die once; you live every day if you choose to." Alex winks at Cintya.
"Well, I don't choose to. I have to go to work tomorrow. See you next time."

Kristy offers her business card to Alex.

"And you, naughty boy, call me if you need a good lawyer to get you out of trouble."
"I have a feeling you might get me into more trouble."

Alex winks at Kristy.

"Well, it is part of what I do."

Kristy smiles seductively at Alex, and she grabs his arms and kisses him on the cheek.

"Bye, handsome."

The rest of the group prepares to leave as well.

"Okay, we are leaving also."
"Cintya, are you coming?"

Alex places his hand on Cintya's lower back and leans towards her, whispering into her ear.

"I don't know about you, but I can have another drink."
"No, I think I will stay for one more drink."
"Okay."

"Bye, Cintya."

"Bye, Alex."

They all leave, and it's just Alex and Cintya who are still at the table.

"Let's get that drink then."

Alex grabs Cintya's hand and starts walking, and she follows his lead. When Alex reaches the bar, he places his empty glass on the counter and keeps walking.

"Leave your glass there."

Alex takes out his phone and orders an Uber.

"Wait, aren't we getting a drink?"

"We are, but I didn't say here now, did I?"

"So, where, then?"

"Somewhere nice, trust me."

Cintya fallows Alex outside of the pub. The two security agents look surprised when they see Alex with a beautiful woman by his side. As Alex passes them, he gives them the business card from Kristy.

"Here you go, fellas. If you ever get into trouble, call this number."

Alex and Cintya get inside the Uber and drive away. One of the security agents snaps back to his senses.

"Yo, where is my ten pounds?"

"How about I give you five and this business card?"

"Nah, bruv, keep the card and give me my ten. You need it more than I do if you keep going to Peckham. Do you get me?"

He starts laughing.

◆ ◆ ◆

Alex and Cintya arrive at The Savoy hotel. Alex gets out of the car first, and then he opens the car door for Cintya.

"We are here, my lady."

"Wow, I have never been to The Savoy before."

They walk inside slowly while Cintya takes a moment to admire the lavish interior. Alex takes the lead again, dragging her gently towards the check-in desk.

"Are we checking in?"

"No."

Alex looks back at her and smiles.

"Hi there, can you please send a bottle of Crystal, caviar, and some strawberries to room 108?"

"Of course, sir."

"Thank you."

Alex leads Cintya towards the lift.

"See, no need to check in."

Alex turns and smiles back at Cintya.

"You really are a naughty boy, aren't you?"

"I know, right?"

They both start laughing as they wait for the lift. Once they get into the room, the champagne arrives swiftly and in a few minutes. They share a glass of champagne out on the balcony, enjoying the view.

"It's nice and quiet here, of course; I don't have to tell you that you have probably been here many times."

Cintya takes a sip from her glass.

"A few times."

Alex smiles at her. A cold breeze passes, sending shivers up on Cintya's back.
"Wow, it's getting cold."
"Here, you can have my jacket."
As Alex takes his jacket off, he accidentally drops his glass. The glass hits the floor and shatters.
"Fuck!"
Alex gives his jacket to Cintya and then goes back inside.
"You, okay?"
"Yes, don't worry, I will clean it."
Alex goes into the bathroom, locks the door, and sits on the toilet.
"Butterfly, butterfly."
Alex starts breathing heavily.
"You can do this. What's the problem?... Sex, that's the problem. Those movies are not explicit, and I don't have much experience... Pornstar, they have a lot of experience. I know a lot of pornstars."
Alex fixes his gaze down at the floor tiles.
"Okay, here we go, ten, nine, eight... ops male pornstars, not female pornstars. I don't know any male pornstars."
"Hey, are you okay in there? Cintya knocks at the bathroom door."
"Yes, I will be out in a minute, love. Just make yourself comfortable." Alex takes out his phone and searches online for male pornstars.
"No, nope... Hey, I have seen this guy before. Okay Jhonny, let's go. Ten, nine, eight..."
Cintya sits on the bed, talking to herself.
"What am I doing here? This is wrong."
Alex opens the bathroom door and comes out.

Cintya gets up from the bed.

"Listen, maybe I should leave-"

Alex starts kissing her passionately and intensely, overpowering her completely. She gives in to him, and he pulls her closer to him and then lifts her up in his arms. She wraps her legs around him. Alex stops for a moment and looks her deep in the eyes.

"I want to see you naked right now. I want to see all of you."

"Yeah, baby, you want to see my butterfly tattoo-"

Alex drops her instantly from his arms. Cintya falls flat on her back on the floor.

"Aw, what the hell!"

"Why did you say that?"

Alex's hands start to shake.

"What?!"

"Why did you say butterfly?"

"I have a butterfly tattoo. What the hell is wrong with you?"

"Fuck!" Alex storms out of the room. Cintya lies down on the floor in pain.

"Where are you going, hey?"

Five seconds later, Alex comes back into the room.

"Hey, help me out. What's wrong with you?"

"I forgot my jacket."

Alex grabs his jacket and storms out again.

"What the fuck is wrong with you? Asshole!"

Alex, waiting alone in the lobby for the lift, hears a soft, unknown voice whispering his name.

"Alex."

Alex turns around, startled, but no one else is in the corridor beside him. The lift doors open, and Alex goes inside.

"Maybe something is wrong with me. I need to change my safety word, that's for sure. The butterfly is not working."

◆ ◆ ◆

The next day, Alex leaves his flat building wearing a black suit and tie. He notices and envelope in his mailbox and takes it out. There is some indiscernible red writing on the envelope. He opens it and sees a bunch of random numbers and letters that don't make any sense.
"Is this some kind of prank? What is this?"
Alex throws it away. He goes back to the same pub, The Eagle. But this time, he arrives late afternoon, around 5 pm, and there is no security at the entrance. He stops in front of the green doors, counts down from ten to one, and then enters. Alex notices two women by the bar; one of them catches his eye. A beautiful redhead around 30 years old wearing a black dress with a red rose pattern. He goes and takes a place at the bar close to the redhead, and she also notices Alex approaching.
"Hi there." Alex winks at her.
"Hi."
Alex then turns toward the bartender.
"I will have a Martini and an Aperol Spritz."
The bartender places the drinks on the counter, and

Alex pays, then turns back at the redhead woman. She looks at him, down at the drinks, and back at Alex.

"Is that for me?"

"Depends."

"On what?"

"Various factors, like if you had a long day at work or if you are beautiful."

"Is that so?"

"You obviously classify for the second point, but I'm afraid you have to tick the first box as well."

Alex smiles.

"I had the longest day of my life, absolutely dreadful."

She smiles back at Alex.

"In that case, please be my guest."

They both reach out and grab their drinks.

"Cheers!"

"Cheers!"

"So, what's your name, or should I call you "the longest day?"

"I'm Anna."

"Nice to meet you. I'm Alex."

"What do you do, Alex?"

"I do my best to make women happy."

"Really?"

"Yeah, it's hard work, but someone has to do it."

"I can imagine."

Anna smiles.

"So, you do your best with single women or married."

"It depends."

"On what?"

"If you are single or married."

"I'm neither."
"How does that work?"
"I'm engaged."
"Well, then, I'm a lucky man."
"You mean my fiancé is a lucky man."
"No, I mean me."
"Why you?"
"My favourite fantasy involves engaged women."
"Really?"
"Yes, no messy break ups, only nights full of passion."
Alex winks at her, and she smiles back at him.
"Usually, I would have kissed you by now."
"What is stopping you?"
"Nothing, nothing, can ever stop me from getting what I want."
"So why not then?"
"You deserve better than this random pub, and you deserve a more romantic setting, perhaps a balcony at a five stars hotel overviewing Thames River at sunset."
Her eyes light up as she bites her lower lip slowly. Alex takes a glance outside the pub through the large windows and looks back at Anna.
"We just might make it in time, but we have to hurry."
Alex grabs her hand and takes the lead.
"You are crazy."
Anna follows him outside with a smile on her face. Alex stops a black cab passing by.
"I need you to trust me."
Alex firmly guides Anna inside the cab, then he climbs in and closes the door. The cab driver is in

his late fifties with white hair, eyeglasses, and a flap cap on his head. The cab driver turns back to the happy couple.

"Are you all right? Where to?"

"I'm alright, and she is stunning."

Alex winks at Anna.

"Can't argue with you there, mate."

"To The Savoy, my good man, make it fast, will you?"

"No worries, I'll get you there in a jiffy."

◆ ◆ ◆

Alex and Anna drink champagne on a balcony and watch the sunset over the Thames River. Anna, playing with her hair in the wind, turns towards Alex.

"The view from here is amazing."

"Yes, it is. Life itself is a poem."

"Are you a fan of poetry?"

"More than a fan, I'm a bit of a poet myself."

"Can I hear one of your poems?"

"Let me choose one perfect for this occasion... Got it, it's called Demon."

Demon

I shall know no defeat.
Standing on my own two feet
I am the Demon Angels pray to
I am the Sun and the Moon
I am the fire in the desert.
The cherry on your dessert
The shadow in your light
The only star in the night
Sweet as vengeance
Sour as justice.

There's a moment of silence as they both stare into each other's eyes with the intensity of two galaxies colliding, releasing an explosion of emotions. Alex pulls Anna closer to him. Her heart starts beating faster and faster in anticipation of wild passion while her lips crave to be kissed.

"I wonder what you taste like."

Alex smiles and gives her a deep, passionate, and ecstatic kiss. Then, he guides her gently back inside the room. He picks her up and throws her on the bed.

"Make yourself comfortable. I will be right back."

Alex goes inside the bathroom and sits on the toilet.

"Butterfly, butterfly. Okay made it so far, and now stage two, the pornstar's experience. Ten, nine, oh wait!"

Alex knocks on the bathroom door.

"Hey, I forgot to ask you if you have any tattoos," shouts Alex.

"What?"

"Tattoos, do you have any?"

"No, why?" Anna asks.

"I... never mind." Alex fixes his gaze down at the bathroom tiles.

"Ten, nine, eight...one."

Anna lies down on the bed when suddenly Alex comes out of the bathroom and fixes his gaze on her like a hawk. He steps towards the bed confidently and begins to kiss her passionately, overpowering her. She surrenders to him completely as Alex undresses her gently. Now completely naked on the bed, Alex suddenly stops the foreplay. He takes a step back and looks her up and down, admiring and savouring her perfect body.

"I want to see you touching yourself."

Alex then takes a glass of champagne, pulls up a chair next to the bed, and sits down to enjoy the show.

"Go ahead, play with yourself."

Alex takes a sip of champagne while Anna obeys his command. She starts caressing her breasts softly and sensually, her right hand moving down her body, slowly teasing her belly button, then moving down to her clitoris, massaging it gently. She then inserts two fingers into her vagina and starts masturbating while seducing Alex with her eyes. She increases her movement speed as she gets closer to climax. Alex stands up, grabs the bottle of champagne, and pours it all over Anna's body. As the cold champagne splashes over her breast, Anna lets herself go completely, arches her back, and rolls her eyes, having an intense orgasm, her legs shaking and heavy breathing. She takes a moment to enjoy that intense pleasure. Then she looks back at Alex with eyes glowing with passion and desire.

"Now get down here on your knees." Alex snaps his fingers, and Anna obeys him like a good girl.

"You are my fuck toy tonight; open your mouth."

Anna obeys him again. Alex takes a sip of champagne and then spits it into her mouth. She gargles it a bit before swallowing it.

"More, I want more."

"Beg me for it."

"Please, Daddy, give me more."

"Such a good girl…"

◆ ◆ ◆

Late in the evening on a Friday night, Dan is casually dressed, walking alone on the pavement in Central London, when he receives a phone call from Alex.

"Hey bro, where are you?" asks Alex.

"I'm on the way, man."

"Hurry up!"

"I'm almost there. I think I can see the pub. Is it the one with an eagle on top?"

"Yes, that's the one, alright, I'm coming outside."

"Okay."

A group of people stands outside the pub on the left and right side of the entrance, smoking and drinking engaged in conversations. On the right side, there are two beautiful women in their late twenties, both wearing evening dresses and high heels, sharing a cigarette. Dan approaches the pub slowly just as Alex steps outside.

"There he is, my brother."

Alex hugs Dan and notices the two beautiful women.

"Can you spare a cigarette?"

Alex turns towards the women.

"Sure."

One of the women hands him a cigarette.

"Since when do you smoke?" Dan asks Alex with a surprised look on his face.

"Since it is my birthday, I will do what I want."

"It's your birthday?"

"Happy birthday!"

"Thanks, how about a kiss for the birthday boy?"

The woman offering Alex a cigarette leans forward to kiss Alex, but at the last second, Alex turns his head, and the kiss lands on his lips.

"Hey!"

The woman pulls back with a smile on her face.

"Hey, hey."

Alex smiles back at her.

"And you, where's my kiss?"

Alex winks at the other woman.

"No, no, I'm not falling for that."

She takes a step back.

"Hey Dan, where is my kiss?" Alex takes a step towards Dan.

"Fuck off, man." Dan pushes Alex back. Everyone starts laughing.

"So disappointing. Where is the love?"

"I don't love you like that, and I barely like you."

"Speaking of love, I invited Jhon and Christine."

"Why? Do you know that they are a couple now?"

"Yeah, they are a lovely couple, unlike you. I don't have a problem with love."

"Man, stop talking about love, and let's get drunk."

"Okay, hey ladies, do you care to join us?"

"Yeah, we would love that."

Apart from Dan, everyone starts laughing as they go inside the pub. They navigate slowly through the sea of people towards a table at the back of the pub where a large group of people are drinking, having a good time, and others standing in a circle. Alex approaches his group of friends with the two beautiful women on each side of his arms.

"Look, everyone, what I have found outside."

Alex joins his friends.

"Lucky you."

Christine gives Alex a jealous look.

"And me."

Dan joins the group also.

"I'm sorry. Do I know you?"

Alex starts laughing.

"Stop playing, jackass, and get me a drink."

Dan smiles back at Alex.

"Get me one too, mate." Jhon snaps his fingers.

"Sure thing, mate, a Jack and Coke, right?"

"Yeah, mate."

"You Dan?"

"Same."

"You ladies?"

"The same why not?"

The two beautiful ladies giggle at each other.

"Great Jack and Coke for everyone coming right up."

Alex goes to the bar and signals one of the bartenders.

"Hey, can I have five Jack and Cokes?"

"Yes, sure."

"But listen, can you do me a favour?" asked Alex.

"What do you need?"

"I'm trying to win a bet tonight, so every time I ask you for Jack and Coke, no matter how many, three, four, or seven, make one of them a double and one only Coke, no Jack. Can you do that for me?"

"I suppose I could."

"Here is a £50 tip for you."

"You can count on me, mate."

The bartender pockets the £50 note, smiling. Alex

returns to his group of friends, gives the Jack and Coke double to Jhon, and keeps the glass of Coke for himself. As the evening progresses, Alex is sober, Dan is a bit tipsy, and Jhon is completely drunk. He stumbles, trying to keep his balance, bumping into people left and right. Christine stands there disappointed, watching Jhon make a fool of himself. Alex approaches Christine and whispers in her ear.

"Hey, are you enjoying yourself?"

"No, not really."

"Why?"

"Well, look at him." Christine points her finger at Jhon.

"Well, personally, I think he is a great dancer." Alex smiles.

"Seriously?"

"Yeah, I have never seen anyone move like that. It must be something new."

"Oh, come on, it is embarrassing. I don't get it; you drank just as much as him, and you are fine."

"Hey, it happens when you drink with the big boys. What more can I say?"

Alex smiles and puts his hand on her lower back.

"When you choose a boy, you end up babysitting."

"A boy!?"

"Well, the evidence speaks for itself. I think you need a man."

"And where can I find a man?"

"It depends; sometimes, a man can be right in front of you."

Alex pulls Christine closer to him and holds her in his arms.

"And what does a man do?" Christine puts her

arms around Alex.
"A man handles his liquor, and that's for sure."
They both smile at each other.
"And what else?"
"A man knows how to take care of your sexy ass."
Alex moves his right hand down on Christine's back and grabs her ass.
"And what else?"
"A man knows how to kiss."
Alex and Christine kiss each other with a burning passion. Alex breaks off the kiss and looks her deep in the eyes.
"A man also knows what he wants."
"And what do you want?"
"I would rather show you."
Alex takes Christine and disappears into the sea of people. Jhon is so drunk that he falls on the floor. Dan comes over and picks him up.
"Come on up, you poor bastard."
Dan drags him over to their reserved table and sits him down on a chair.
"Has anyone seen Christine or Alex?"
"No."
"No."
"I think they went to the toilets."
"Can someone tell Alex I'm leaving?"
"What?"
"What?"
"Never mind, I will tell him myself."
"What? What did he say?"
Dan goes to the toilet; the male toilet is empty, but one of the stall doors is closed.
"Alex, are you in here, man?"

"Yes, why?"
Alex catches his breath.
"I'm leaving."
"What, why?"
"I'm done. I'm wasted, man."
"Come on, bro, don't leave."
"Open the door, and let me see you before I go."
Dan force opens the stall door, and to his surprise, he sees Alex with his pants down and Christine down on her knees giving him oral.
"Wow, bro!"
"Sorry, sorry."
Dan panics and tries to close the door.
"It's fine, don't worry about it." Alex smiles.
"I wanted to wish you a happy birthday again, but I see you are already happy."
"I am the happiest man ever."
Alex winks at Dan.
"Okay, I'm gone."
"Bro, shut the door!"
Alex shouts back at Dan, but the loud music cancels his voice. Dan doesn't hear him as he walks away. Alex leans back against the wall and takes a deep breath. The toilet lights flicker while the music slowly fades away, and a complete silence settles in. The sound of the clock ticking breaks the silence.
"Tik Tok, Tik Tok."
An unknown voice calls Alex.
"Alex, Alex."
"Who's there?"
Alex is startled by the voice, pulls up his trousers, and gets out of the toilet stall, desperately looking

left and right.

"Alex, what's wrong?"

Christine breaks the silence while getting back on her feet.

"Did you hear that?"

Alex turns towards her with a frightened look on his face.

"Hear what?"

Alex catches a glimpse of himself in the mirror when the music comes back at full blast and startles him.

"We should go back."

Alex rushes out of the toilet, leaving Christine behind. Christine shouts his name back at him, and for a moment, Christine's voice and the unknown voice overlap.

"Alex!"

"Alex!"

◆ ◆ ◆

On Friday evening, Alex, wearing a black suit and tie, exits from Stratford Station, turns left up the stairs, and crosses the bridge to Westfield Shopping Centre. The large pedestrian bridge that leads to the Shopping Centre has tall glass walls on each side, giving a perfect view over the train station. The Shopping Centre has three floors and over 300 retailers, a variety of restaurants and food courts, a cinema, and a casino. Alex avoids the main entrance and decides to take the street entrance to the Aspers Casino. He takes the first right and passes a few wooden benches, a ping pong table, and a few outdoor restaurants and café terraces by the outdoor sitting area. People walk by slowly in every direction like waves merging with each other, pushing and pulling in opposite directions. Frustrated and anxious, Alex is forced to slow down and walk at the same pace as everyone else. People's voices and the music from an outdoor pub merge into a perfect harmony of urban noise. Alex reaches the entrance to the Casino, where two security agents escort a man outside from the Casino. The man is in his late thirties, drunk and loud, causing a scene. Some people stop in their tracks to witness the event, hoping it will escalate into a fight.

"Come on, let's have it, you fucking prick!"

The drunk man takes off his shirt and takes on a fight stance. One of the security guards intervenes to calm him down.

"Sir, we can't let you in as you are intoxicated. Please leave, or we will be forced to call the police."

Alex approaches the entrance cautiously; the other security agent notices him.

"Good evening, sir. Are you going in?"

"I was thinking about it."

"Go ahead, don't worry about our friend here; he is upset with us, not you."

"I think he is upset with the world in general."

"You might be right, but what can you do?"

"Keep calm and carry on, I suppose."

Alex smiles at the security agent while passing through the doors.

"You should tell him that."

The security guy smiles back at Alex. Inside the building, there is another security agent standing behind a small reception stand near the lift.

"Good evening. Sir, can I see an ID?"

"Yeah, sure," says Alex.

The security agent scans Alex's ID and gives it back to him.

"Is this your first time, or are you a member?"

"First time."

"Okay, welcome to Aspers Casino. Take the lift up to the second floor, and the reception is on your left. You can buy chips or cash for the slot machines. We also have a terrace bar. Enjoy your evening, sir."

"Cheers, mate."

The lift doors open, and Alex steps out on the Casino floor and stops for a moment being mesmerized by the gambling atmosphere. The casino is packed full of people seduced by the fast life and easy money, like a mirage in the desert but with colourful lights. The red carpet with a yellow flower pattern gives a feeling of vertigo. Casino is this magical place where hopes and dreams are being crushed daily, yet people come back to it again and again, addicted to pleasure and pain. Alex walks past the slot machines on his right and notices a beautiful redhead wearing a leopard print dress sitting at one of the machines. They make eye contact for a second as Alex passes by. On the opposite side, on the left, there are a few roulettes and a blackjack table. At the end of the roulette tables on the left is the entrance to the bar, a large open entrance with the name Tanzibar written above the entrance with LED lights. Inside the bar on the opposite side of the entrance, there is a large TV screen showing a football match, giving the vibe of a classic British Pub but with better furniture. Wooden floors and tables surrounded by brown leather chairs and blue cushioned chairs. Next to the bar on the left is the entrance to the poker tables area of the casino. The blue surface poker table is surrounded by black leather chairs shining bright under the blue neon light from the ceiling. Alex takes a moment to decide which table to join when he notices one on the far right with only four players: a skinny old geezer with gold jewellery and a gold front tooth wearing a blue suit and gold frame eyeglasses., a punk girl with pink hair, an Arsenal football fan wearing a football jersey and a guy with black sunglasses. Alex goes to the toilet and locks himself inside one of the stalls.

"Okay, someone who plays poker. I don't know any poker players, so let's google it. Shit, no signal. I guess I'm stuck with James Bond again. Okay, here goes nothing ten, nine, eight..."

Alex emerges from the toilet, walking casually and confidently approaching the poker table.

"Good evening, everyone. Do you mind if I join in?"

"Of course, sir, please."

The dealer points at the empty chair across from the old geezer with the gold tooth.

"The game is Texas Hold'em; you are starting as the small blind."

"Okay, thank you."

Alex takes a moment to study the other players as the dealer deals the cards. The old geezer and the pink-haired girl are in the lead with the most chips, while the Arsenal fan and the guy with sunglasses are close to losing. Alex turns toward the Arsenal fan.

"So, you're an Arsenal fan."

"What gave me away?"

"In all honesty, I would have guessed even without the T-shirt."

"How so?"

"By looking at your chips, it seems you are used to losing."

"Don't be so sure about that."

"This is what I love about football fans: they never lose hope, even when it's hopeless."

Alex smiles while the football fan grinds his teeth. All throughout the game, every time the Arsenal fan bets, Alex folds; when the football fan folds, Alex raises the bet. The dealer reveals The Flop, the first three cards, and the football fan places a bet, giving Alex a provocative look.

"You have been running from me all night long."

"Just like the football during a match."

Alex smiles back at him.

"Very funny, what can I say?"

"Warm-up is over; time to play, call you mate."

"Finally, you found your courage."

"It's time I put you out of your misery, mate."

The other players fold. The dealer reveals The

Turn, which is the fourth card. The football fan raises again.

"Time to make you sweat."

"The coach never sweats, mate, check."

Alex lays back on his chair. The dealer reveals The River as the final card.

"It's time to retire, coach, all in."

"I think you need to go back on the bench; you are not premier league material."

"You are out, coach; here are three yellow cards for you."

The football fan reveals three of a kind, three sevens. Alex looks down at the cards on the table and then back at his opponent.

"Nice, here is a red card, and you are out."

Alex reveals a flush.

"Fuck!"

The football fan jumps up from his seat. The dealer tries to console him.

"Sir, please try and remain calm."

"Fuck you, fuck you both. You are probably working together, and I know it, fucking twats."

The dealer signals the security to escort him out. The manager comes over to the table.

"Is everyone alright? My apologies, but we don't tolerate this kind of behaviour here."

"It's alright, no worries."

"Do you need a break, or do you wish to carry on?"

"Yeah, it's okay, so let's play."

"We are good as long as people keep their testosterone in check."

The girl with pink hair gives Alex a dirty look. The dealer carries on.

"My apologies, everyone. I may have been responsible for this mess. I need to accept people for who they are, you know. Some people are football fans, and other movie fans like Neo over here. Am I right, buddy?"

Alex nods at the guy with sunglasses.

"You are doing it again."

The pink-haired girl rolls her eyes.

"It's okay, let's play."

The guy with sunglasses is unfazed by Alex's rude comments.

"See, he is alright; he is a Zen master; nothing throws him off. He can see through the cards, but he's still losing. We really are in the Matrix."

Alex smiles. As the game progresses, the guy with sunglasses decides to risk it all on one hand and starts betting before the flop is revealed. Alex takes him on while the other two players fold.

"I see someone is feeling lucky, check and I will raise you £200."

"Fine, check and raise £300 for you. How do you like that?"

"I love it, mate, check and raise you £500."

"Fine, I guess I'm all in, then."

The sunglasses guy throws his last chips in the pot.

"Well, then show me the cards. I'm guessing Neo has already seen them."

Alex addresses the dealer. The dealer reveals the cards. "Neo" has two pairs, and Alex wins with a full house.

"Neo buddy, I think you need an upgrade. You better go home and reload."

Alex laughs at his own joke while "Neo" walks away

with his head down.

"And now there were three."

Alex winks at the pink-haired girl.

"Forget it; your tricks don't work for me."

She rolls her eyes back at Alex.

"Relax, love, like all men out there, I'm just going to ignore you."

The pink-haired girl gives him an angry look while Alex smiles triumphantly. Alex starts playing chaotically, raising the bet a few times, then folds, doing everything possible to ruin the flow of the game. For most of the game, the old geezer quietly observes the other players, but now, even though he is a bit aggravated, he starts tapping on the table with two fingers every time Alex throws the game away. While the old geezer keeps his discomfort to himself, the pink girl verbally attacks Alex every chance she gets, and Alex ignores her completely. Sensing that she is almost at her breaking point, Alex takes her head on.

"Raise £100."

"Why are you doing this? Are you going to fold again?"

The pink-haired girl gives Alex an angry look while he counts his chips.

"Fold."

The old geezer throws his cards on the table.

"You better not fold again, check and raise you £200."

The pink-haired girl angrily throws some chips on the pot.

"Check and raise you £300."

Alex slowly adds chips to the pot.

"Oh my god, I hate you so much. I just know you will fold again. I'm all in. I swear to God if you fold again."

"Check, all in."

Alex calmly adds all his chips to the pot.

"Finally, one of us got to go. I can't take it anymore."

Alex wins with four of a kind.

"Motherfucker!" the pink-haired girl growled.

The pink-haired girl grids her teeth as she leaves the table, pacing toward the exit.

"Did you hear something?" Alex smiles at the dealer.

"Just you and me now, no worries. I will try to make it quick if you are tired."

Alex winks at the old man.

"Do us a favour and worry about yourself, alright, son?"

"Someone is a bit grumpy today."

"Be careful now, or you might lose that silver tongue of yours to my sharp knife. You are barking at the wrong tree, son."

"Easy now, just making conversation."

"Do us a favour and put a sock on it. And you there get a move on. I don't plan on spending my night with you." The old man snaps his finger at the dealer.

"We don't tolerate any abuse here, sir."

The dealer stops shuffling the cards.

"Do your job, mate, and don't worry about me."

Alex takes a look at his two cards.

"I feel lucky."

Alex bets £500 before the dealer reveals the Flop.

"We'll see about that, check."
The old man also bets £500. The dealer reveals the Flop.
"Oh, I should have bought a lottery ticket, raise you £500."
"I see what you're doing, check."
The old man throws some chips on the pot.
"Do you want to know what I see?"
"Don't really care, son."
"I see a royal flush down there."
"You are bluffing."
"Raise you another £500; how's that for bluffing?"
"Do you think you can push me around, son? Trust me, you will be the one shaking like a leaf. Check and raise you another £500."
"Be careful now; you don't want your blood pressure to get too high. Check, here is your £500."
The dealer reveals the Turn the fourth card.
"I'm buying a lottery ticket after this. This is going to be a humiliating defeat on your part. You might as well fold."
"Bluffing doesn't work on me, son."
"I didn't bluff all night, so why would I start now? You know what? Let's end it quickly. I'm all in."
"You are bluffing."
The old man snaps his fingers nervously.
"There is only one way to find out."
Alex stares into the old man's eyes, deep into his very soul. With such a powerful gaze that the old man has never experienced, Alex has completely changed from this charming young man into a ruthless assassin, sending shivers up the spine. The old man feels like his life depends on his next

move; he feels like he is gambling with his life at this very moment. He is having a staring contest with death itself, and if he blinks, then it is "game over."

"Sir, are you in?"

The dealer brings the old man back on his feet.

"What, um yeah, no, fold."

The old man, still a bit dizzy, throws down his cards.

"Good call."

Alex starts collecting all the chips.

"Okay, let's see it."

"See what?"

"The royal flush."

"Who said that I have a royal flush?"

"You did."

"I believe my exact words were: I see a royal flush down there; I didn't say I have a royal flush now, did I?"

"What are you saying, son? You played me?"

"I guess that's what happens when you get old; you are not as sharp as before."

Alex gets up and goes to the bar. While waiting for the bartender, the beautiful redhead with the leopard dress passes by.

"Love your dress."

Alex winks at her.

"Thanks."

She smiles at him.

"Do you care to join me?"

"My husband might not like that."

"Come on, one drink doesn't hurt anyone."

"Oh, honey, clearly you didn't have one with me."

"I think I can manage." Alex turns to the bartender. "A Jin and tonic and one Aperol Spritz for this gorgeous troublemaker."

The old man and four thugs surround Alex. He sees them in the mirror on the wall.

"What can I get for you boys?" Alex turns around.

"A protein shake, perhaps."

"You took my money, and you're trying to take my wife away."

The old man takes a step forward.

"It can't hurt to try."

Alex smiles back at the old man.

"Yes, it can, son."

"You lads have fun." The redhead woman walks away.

"It's not going to be fun without you."

Alex winks at her as she walks away.

"Let me handle this, governor."

One of the four thugs grabs Alex by the collar.

"Jimmy, I'm the brain, and you are the muscle, and it worked out great so far. Now, why do you want to change that?"

"Sorry, governor I-"

"Are you some sort of gangster?"

Alex cuts Jimmy off.

"Jimmy!"

The old man snaps his fingers, and Jimmy punches Alex in the stomach. Alex crouches down in pain. For a moment, everything goes silent, and the lights start to flicker. Then, the sound of a clock breaks the silence; "Tik Tok, Tik Tok." An unknown voice whispers his name; "Alex."

"I'm not a gangster; I'm Larry Gold. I'm... Hey, look

at me."

Larry snaps his fingers, and Jimmy grabs Alex by the back of his neck and pulls him back to his feet. Alex comes back to his senses, and the sound of the clock and the unknown voice fade away.

"I'm Larry Gold. I'm a businessman, and crime is my business, got it?"

"Yep."

Alex catches his breath. The bartender notices that Alex is in trouble, but before he can say anything, Jimmy gives him a menacing look.

"Is there something wrong with your eyes, mate?"

Jimmy takes a step closer to the bar.

"No."

"Then why are you looking at me?"

The bartender puts his head down and pretends to fix a drink.

"Alright, that's enough."

Larry signals Jimmy to back off.

"You, Royal Flush, what's your name?"

"Alex."

"Do us a favour, Alex, and fuck off!"

Larry snaps his fingers, and Alex walks away slowly, holding his stomach with his left hand. Larry turns to Jimmy.

"This bloke gets in more trouble than Bugs Bunny. What do I always say? One man's problem is another man's profit. Put a hound on his fluffy tail, and let's see how deep the rabbit hole goes."

"Sure thing, governor."

Jimmy turns back to one of the gangsters.

"Dave, get on it."

◆ ◆ ◆

Alex is determined not to let the casino incident ruin his night, so he heads to Mayfair, one of the posh areas of London. Filled with confidence and cash in his pockets, he enters the Coburg Bar located in the 5-star Connaught Hotel. The Coburg Bar is a classy and glamorous bar with a chandelier hanging from the ceiling, a fireplace, and vintage furniture. Alex walks towards the bar to order himself a drink and notices a beautiful blonde woman with blue eyes in her late 40s, wearing a lowcut black dress with ruby necklaces and gold earrings and her long blonde hair cascading over her shoulders. She is alone, sipping on a cocktail while her eyes scan the room in a very subtle way. She notices Alex and their eyes lock for a second before she turns her gaze away to the fireplace. For some reason, Alex is more attracted to the ruby necklace than to the beautiful woman. It is like the small red stone has put him under a curse, and he continues to stare at it for a few seconds more, causing him to bang his knee on a bar stool. Alex leans on the bar, trying to mask his pain, and signals one of the bartenders, hoping the woman didn't notice his clumsiness.

"Good evening, sir. What can I get you?"

"Vodka martini."

"A fine choice, sir."

"It seems to be a quiet evening, well, apart from that blonde storm over there. What can you tell me about her?"

"She is a guest at the hotel, but I'm afraid she is not looking for company this evening. A few gentlemen have already tried and failed."

"That's because she is looking for the 'right' company."

Alex winks at the bartender.

"In that case, enjoy your evening, sir."

The bartender hands over the martini to Alex.

"I intend to."

Alex turns around, making eye contact with the blonde woman. He smiles and raises his glass. She smiles back at him and points at an empty chair at her table. Alex walks over and sits down.

"How's your evening?"

"A bit boring, how about you?"

"Mine just turned better about five seconds ago."

Alex winks at her.

"What is the world coming to, seeing a beautiful woman like you sitting by herself? Where are all the men?"

"That's a good question."

"I see a few of them here tonight, but-"

"I don't see any."

"Really, any?"

"One perhaps too early to tell."

She smiles at Alex.

"I detect an accent in your English; you are from Eastern Europe."

"Further east."

"Ah, Russia, of course, is where I should have known."

"How so?"

"Russian people are straightforward, and the women are strong and beautiful. What's your name?"

"Katja, you also have an East European accent."

"I'm from Romania, and I'm Alex, by the way."

"Alex is short for Alexander; we also have that name in Russia."

"No, it is just Alex."

"I see it makes sense; after all, you were a communist country and part of the Soviet Union."

"Yeah, our countries share some history together. We didn't like each other that much, did we?"

"No, we didn't."

"We should do something about that."

"What do you suggest?"

"I will get us a bottle of Vodka, and we are going to find out where we stand in terms of love or war."

Alex winks at her.

"You seem to know the way to a Russian woman's heart; however, one bottle might not be enough."

Katja smiles at Alex.

"If I must die on the battlefield, so be it."

Alex smiles back at her, then walks away while Katja can't help but laugh. As the evening progresses, Alex and Katja are the only ones left in the bar, laughing and telling jokes as they are halfway to the second bottle of Vodka. Katja reaches out her arm and touches Alex on his leg in a seductive and gentle manner.

"So, Alexander, what do you do for a living?"

"It's Alex, not Alexander."
"No, no, it's Alexander. That's the original name, and that's what I will call you."
"Okay, I guess, as long as you don't call me Jimmy." They both laugh out loud.
"What kind of name is that? That's not a man's name."
"I know, right?"
"So, Alexander, what do you do?"
"I'm a writer and a poet."
"I love poetry. Tell me one."
Alex reaches out, grabs her chair, and pulls her closer to him.
"I can tell you this poem called Eternal."

Eternal

Love and hate are eternal nemesis.
In the garden of blood, roses
Betting my life on a kiss
Losing myself in the eternal bliss.

Alex kisses Katja with a vibrant passion, their lips colliding against each other like two armies on the battlefield, their tongues fiercely fighting each other, creating an explosion of emotions, love, and hate, eternal enemies becoming lovers for the first time and releasing so much sexual energy that their bodies move involuntarily trying to overpower each other knocking off the table the empty bottle of Vodka. The sound of the bottle breaking acts like a cease-fire order, putting an end to the fierce kiss.

"I have a room at The Savoy."

Alex winks at Katja.

"I have a room upstairs."

Katja smiles and rubs Alex's leg seductively.

"Even better."

◆ ◆ ◆

A hotel room door slams open as Katja and Alex enter, kissing and battling each other. They lose their balance and fall on the floor, with Katja landing on Alex.

"I want to ride your cock."
Katja whispers into Alex's ear.
"Let me get the door first."
"Fuck the door."
"I prefer women."
"What?"
Alex pushes Katja off him, gets up, and shuts the door. Then turns back at Katja.
"Okay, now let's get you to bed, shall we?"
Alex extends his arm to help her get up, but Katja grabs him by his trousers instead.
"Give me your cock."
"Wow, behave yourself if you want it. Follow me to the bed."
Alex slaps her hand away and walks toward the bed. Katja gets up and jumps on his back.
"Give me that cock. Give it to me."
"Jesus."
Alex struggles to keep his balance, barely making it to the bed. They both fall on the bed and then the "battle" begins, both take their clothes off. Completely naked, Katja gets on top.
"You stay there, don't move."
"Do I have a choice?"
"No, you don't."
Katja grabs Alex's penis, spits on it, and then sinks her teeth in the tip of his penis.
"Hey, no biting."

Alex flinches.

"No biting; what kind of sex is that?"

"No dick biting, okay?"

"Fine."

Katja starts sucking his penis deeply and passionately while making eye contact with Alex.

"Fuck me, that feels good."

"I haven't started fucking you yet."

Katja spits on his penis again, then gets on top and rides Alex hard, jumping up and down his cock.

"Fuuuck!"

"Yeah, baby, give me that cock."

As the passion between them grows, Alex is distracted by the ruby necklace, and he can't help but stare at the jewellery while Katja goes crazy on his dick. Suddenly, Alex grabs Katja by the hips and rolls her over. Now Alex gets on top of Katja and starts pounding her while focusing his gaze on the ruby. His right arm moves slowly up across Katja's body from her belly button up to her breast, then up to the necklace, and just as he's about to touch it, Katja grabs his arm and places it on her neck.

"Yeah, baby, choke me."

Alex squeezes her neck between his fingertips.

"Do you like that?"

"Yeah, baby fuck me harder."

Alex pounds her faster and harder.

"Fuck I'm going to cum."

"Yeah, baby, give it to me cum inside me."

Katja wraps her legs around Alex, grabs Alex by the back of his neck with her left hand, and pulls him closer.

"Fuuck!"

"Give it to me, cum inside me!"

They both climax at the same time; Katja arches her back and rolls her eyes while Alex snatches her necklace and hides it under a pillow...

In the morning, Alex is the first to wake up, watches Katja sleep, and then dresses up in a hurry. He opens the door, takes one step out, and then suddenly remembers something. He goes back, softly slides his hand under a pillow, snatches the ruby necklace, and runs out.

◆ ◆ ◆

Alex is driving around late at night when he spots a petrol station. He stops on the opposite side of the road where he can have a clear view of the petrol station. There are no customers inside, only two employees working on the graveyard shift. No cars are passing by on the road; it is all peace and quiet. Alex takes a deep breath, then opens the glove compartment, pulls out a gun, and slides a ski mask over his head. He then gets out of the car and goes inside the petrol station.

"Give me all the money now!"

The two employees were caught by surprise. They just froze, standing still.

"Give me all the fucking cash!"

Alex smacks one of the employees and then points

at the cash register.

"Open it now!"

The employee's hands shake as he opens the register and gives all the money to Alex. He pockets the money, runs out, gets in his car, takes the mask off, and drives away fast. One of the employees follows Alex outside and sees him driving away, their eyes locked for a split second.

"Fuck, he saw my face and my car registration number."

Alex punches the steering wheel. He keeps driving, ignoring the traffic lights like a bank robber, and then pulls up on a dark, quiet street and parks between two cars.

"This is bad, really bad. How am I going to get out of this? He saw my face; he saw my car. I'm so fucked right now."

Alex notices a bin under a streetlight. He gets out of the car and throws everything away: the mask, the gun, and all the money.

"This is so messed up."

Alex rubs his temples. The streetlight starts to flicker, and the sound of the clock ticking breaks the silence.

"Tick tock, tick tock."

An unknown voice whispers Alex's name.

"Alex, Alex."

"Who's there?"

Alex looks desperately left and right, but there is no one on the street.

"I have to reset. Butterfly! Butterfly!"

The unknown voice shouts his name.

"Alex!"

In a blink of an eye, Alex is back in his flat, sitting

on his sofa, staring at the ruby necklace in the palm of his hand. Suddenly, he jumps up.

"What the fuck happened; how did I get back home? Was I dreaming?"

He takes another look at the necklace.

"I have to get rid of this thing."

◆ ◆ ◆

Alex walks inside a luxurious jewellery store in London. The Turkish owner wears a black and gold shirt, a black vest, and gold frame glasses. The last two buttons of his shirt are open, revealing a gold chain on his neck, covered in gold jewellery, a gold watch on his right arm, a gold bracelet on his left wrist, and gold rings on most of his fingers. Alex browses around for a bit, then approaches the store owner.

"Hi."

"See anything that you like?" The store owner asks.

"I could ask you the same."

"What do you mean?"

"The sign says you buy and sell jewellery."

"Yes, you wish to sell something."

"It depends on what you can offer me for this."
Alex places the ruby necklace on the glass counter. The owner picks it up and studies it for a bit.
"Nice work. I'm guessing it may be Russian."
"Maybe."
"My friend, I can offer you £10,000."
"Ok, it's a deal."
"I just need to see some ID, and I will be more than happy to take it."
"Yeah, about that, I just remembered I forgot my ID at home."
"That is a problem, my friend."
"Yeah, it's a shame, I know, but…"
"You can go home and come back, and we are open until 8 pm."
"Yeah, you see, I live far away; perhaps you could do me a favour."
"My friend, no ID, it's a problem for me. Without ID, I can offer you only £6000 in cash."
"£6000."
"My friend, it's a good deal, take it."
"Okay, fine."

◆ ◆ ◆

Alex arrives at his flat building, and just as he is about to enter, two massive Russian guys snatch him, throw him in the back of a black Mercedes, and drive away. The car arrives at the construction site of an apartment building. The Russians drag Alex all the way up to the top floor, where a Russian businessman waits for him. He is a tall, well-built man around 60 years old with white hair and a beard with a scar above his right eye, and he is wearing a dark blue striped suit. The businessman exchanges some words in Russian with his men and then stands there silent like an executioner ready to swing his axe. Alex breaks the silence.

"What's this? Who are you? Listen, I don't know what's going on, but you have the wrong man."
"You fucked my wife."
"No, I will never do something like that."
"Yes, you did."
"No, of course not."
"Yes."
"No."
"Yes."
"No."

"Suka blyat." The businessman punches Alex in the abdomen.
"You steal jewels, necklace ruby."
"Well…" Alex, catching his breath.
"Give it back."
"Well, you see, I don't have it."
"Bring it back here tomorrow."
"It's weird that you care more about that than me sleeping with your wife."
"My wife likes young boys. I like hookers. Who cares? But the necklace belonged to my babushka."
"Who?"
"Babushka."
"What is that, your dog?"
"No, no dog. It's how you say?"
The businessman speaks with his bodyguards in Russian, repeating the word babushka a couple of times. The bodyguards look back at him helplessly.
"Niet, boss."
The businessman, losing his patience, shouts at Alex.
"Babushka is babushka! It's the old lady."
"Ah, you mean grandmother."
"Yes, babushka. Bring the necklace here tomorrow by 8 pm."
"I'm sorry, but I sold it."
"Suka blyat, get it back."
"I will you have my word, I promise."
"Your word?"
"Yes."
"In Russia, we have this saying; "Yesli sobirayesh'sya nazyvat' sebya molochnym gribom, zalezay v korzinu!"

The Russian turns to his bodyguards.
"Hey, translate to him."
The two bodyguards raise their shoulders up.
"Niet boss."
"Suka blyat."
"It's okay. Never mind, I think I get it."
Alex tries to leave, but the businessman pulls him back.
"No, wait."
The businessman takes out his mobile phone, uses Google Translate, and then passes the phone to Alex.
"Here, read this."
Alex takes the phone and reads it out loud.
"If you are going to call yourself a milk mushroom, get in the basket!"
"Do you now understand?"
The businessman puts the phone back in his pocket.
"Yeah, I don't know what the fuck that means."
"Suka blyat! Necklace you steal."
"Well"
"Bring it back, or you fly."
"What?!"
"You fly."
The businessman shouts something in Russian at his bodyguards. They immediately grab Alex and hold his head down over the edge of the building.
"My necklace or you fly."
"Okay, okay, I will bring it back, I swear."
The businessman signs to his bodyguards to pull Alex back up. He looks him dead in the eyes, and then he points at his wristwatch.

"At 8 pm, you be here with babushka necklace."
"Got it. I will be here, I swear."
Alex's legs were shaking.

◆ ◆ ◆

Alex runs back to the jewellery store just about closing time. The owner locks the store when Alex comes running.

"Wait, wait!"
Alex catches his breath.
"Hey, my friend, you have something else to sell."
"No, the necklace, I want it back. Here is your money, please. I need it back."
"Sorry, my friend, you are too late."
"Come on, man, it will take five seconds just to open the store. Do you want more money or what?"
"No, my friend, you are too late because I already sold it."
"You're serious, to whom?"
"Some old guy."
"How can I find him? Do you have his contact

info?"

"No, he paid cash and left."

"Fuck!" screamed Alex.

"Hey, my friend, sometimes you have good days; sometimes you have bad days."

"And sometimes they mix, and you are totally fucked."

Alex walks away with his head down.

◆ ◆ ◆

Another glamorous evening at The Savoy Hotel, Alex walks into the restaurant feeling like an outsider, like a cameraman, capturing a glimpse of the rich and famous luxurious lifestyle where the sky is the limit. Envy and jealousy creep into his soul as the high life unfolds before his eyes with expensive champagne pouring over diamonds and fake smiles. A beautiful blonde girl in her twenties wearing a yellow summer dress catches his attention. Alex is completely mesmerized by her, this angel who stops time and captures Alex's soul while his heart beats faster. He is completely lost in this moment that feels like an eternity of bliss and happiness. Love at first sight, this ancient curse has fallen upon Alex, and his body moves unconscious, never taking his eyes off her. He blocks out everything and everyone. Even though he is some distance from her, he can hear her voice and her sweet laughter, like a mermaid singing in the distance. Walking in this zombie state, he bumps into a waiter who drops his tray. The sound of glasses smashing and breaking on the floor awakes him from his trance and also puts him in the spotlight as everyone turns and looks at him. Embarrassed, he apologizes immediately and runs to the toilet. He locks himself in one of the toilet stalls.

"That was so embarrassing; come on, Alex, get it together. If you can't, then someone else can. Ten, nine, eight…one."

Alex emerges from the toilet filled with confidence and walks straight to the beautiful blonde girl's table. She is accompanied by two other girls; they are engaged in conversation while enjoying a bottle of Cristal Champagne. Alex interrupts their conversation.

"Evening ladies."

"IIi."

"Hello."

Alex turns toward the blonde girl.

"I love your shoes."

"Thanks, me too."

"I have a pair just like that."

"Really?"

"Granted, they belonged to an ex-girlfriend."

"Is that so?"

"Here is what I don't understand: she loved them, and you say you love them. So, let me ask you, would you ever consider throwing them away?"

"No, why would I throw them away?"

"Of course not. That will be crazy, right?"

"Yeah."

"See, my ex went crazy one day, and she threw

them away."
"Really?!"
"Granted, she was aiming at my head, but still."
"Oh my god, what did you do?"
"Nothing."
"Yeah, right."
"I still say it's because of the shoes. I am worried about you. Be careful walking around in those shoes. You might be next."
"Yeah, right, what about you and that poor waiter?"
"What waiter?"
"A moment ago, you knocked him over."
"Nonsense, I just gave him a tip, that's all."
"It's more like a nudge."
"It was a heavy tip that made him lose his balance."
Everyone starts laughing.
"So, what's your name?"
The blonde girl asks Alex while playing with her hair.
"Alex."
"I'm Beatrice, and this is Laura and Katie."
"Nice to meet you all. May I join you?"
"Yes."
"So, Alex, what do you do besides upsetting girls?"
"I lie to them." Alex takes a seat.
"You are terrible. What do you do for fun, then?"
Beatrice grabs Alex's arm.
"That is fun." Alex smiles.
"You are such an asshole."
Beatrice lets go of his arm and rolls her eyes.
"I know, right?"
Alex smiles back at her while the other two girls

burst out laughing,

"What's the biggest lie you ever told a girl?"

Laura asks Alex while reaching for her champagne glass.

"I once told a girl I have a small penis. Now, that was a big lie." Alex winks at Beatrice.

"You really are terrible."

Beatrice touches Alex's arm while laughing.

"What do you do for a living?"

Katie asks Alex.

"I'm a writer of poetry."

"Really, tell me a poem."

Beatrice jumps in her chair excitedly.

"Only if you ask me nicely."

Alex smiles at Beatrice.

"Oh, come on seriously."

"It's okay, I can wait."

Alex leans back in his chair. The other two girls start to beg.

"Come on, please."

"Please tell us."

"And you?"

Alex turns toward Beatrice.

"And me what?"

"Come on, Beatrice, don't be like that."

Laura and Katie pressure Beatrice to say please.

"Hey, you were supposed to be my friends."

"Oh, come on, Beatrice, stop being such a spoiled princess."

"Well, hello, I am a…"

"Never mind; just play along this time."

"Fine."

Beatrice rolls her eyes and then turns to Alex.

"Will you be so kind as to recite one of your poems for us?"

"You forgot to say please, but fine, I will take it. Now let me see... I think you will love this one, "The Hunter.""

Alex looks Beatrice deep in her eyes as he recites the poem...

The Hunter

Driven by hunger
I am the hunter.
Looking for my prey
Better run no time to pray.
Hiding in plain sight
Can hear your heartbeat,
A mile away.
Got you in my sight,
Up on your feet
Let the hunt begin.
Nothing sweet like this
Hunting for your kiss.

After a moment of silence, Beatrice feels butterflies in her stomach, and her heart beats faster. Losing herself in Alex's eyes, she bites her lower lip while fantasizing about kissing him. Laura breaks the silence.

"That was a great poem, alright."

"Yeah, it was."

Beatrice snaps back to reality and takes a sip of champagne.

"Okay, it's time to go. Come on, girls."

Beatrice bangs on the table with the palm of her hand.

"Well, that's a shame."

Alex smiles.

"Why do you want to leave already?"

Laura asks Beatrice.

"We have an early day tomorrow, remember? So I'm going up to my room. We are going up."

Beatrice fumbles around, getting ready to leave, and drops her purse.

"Are you staying here at The Savoy?"

Alex picks up the purse and hands it over to Beatrice.

"Yeah, she is staying in room 109."

Laura snitches on Beatrice as she gets up from her chair.

"Laura!"

Beatrice gives Laura a mean look.

"I'm staying at 108, and we are practically neighbours. Maybe I will swing by for a nightcap."
"My door will be locked," Beatrice replies to Alex without looking at him.
"Well, in that case, I have no choice but to swing from the balcony," Alex also gets up from his chair.
"I would love to see that."
Laura touches Alex on his shoulder.
"Let's go already."
Beatrice leaves, followed by her friends.
"Bye, Alex."
"Nice to meet you."
Laura and Katie say goodbye while Beatrice keeps walking without looking back.
"Good night, ladies. It's always a pleasure."

◆ ◆ ◆

Beatrice enters her room and sits on her bed, looking at the balcony occasionally. She turns on the TV and browses through the channels, with one eye on the TV and one on the balcony door. She takes a deep breath, throws away the remote, opens the balcony door, and sticks her head out. Looking left and right, she doesn't see anyone else.

"I knew he was lying," she thought as she stepped outside to enjoy the view.
"Men, they're all the same."
She turns around, and just as she is about to enter back into her room, a balcony door opens from the room next to her, and Alex steps out with a

champagne bottle and two glasses. They both see each other.

"What are you doing here?"

Beatrice takes a step closer to the balcony edge.

"I came out to enjoy the view."

"With a bottle of champagne and two glasses?"

"What can I say? I might have a drinking problem."

Alex smiles.

"Yeah, maybe."

Beatrice smiles back at him.

"Or maybe I had a feeling that I might find you out here."

Alex places the champagne and the glasses on a small table.

"Is that so?"

"The evidence speaks for itself."

A moment of silence as Alex pours the champagne.

"So, are you going to swing from the balcony?"

Beatrice breaks the silence.

"I'm not drunk enough yet."

Alex looks down over the balcony and then hands one of the glasses to Beatrice. Their balconies are close to each other, within arm's reach.

"Cheers!"

"Cheers!"

They both take a sip, and Alex turns his gaze away.

"London is beautiful at night."

"Yeah, it is."

"But then again, so are you."

Alex turns back to Beatrice and stares into her eyes.

"Thanks."

Beatrice blushes a bit.

"What colour are your eyes?"
Alex stares deeper into her eyes.
"They are blue."
"They look green."
"They're blue."
"They don't look blue."
"Yes, they are. It's just the night light."
"You are lying."
"No, I'm not."
"Yes, you are."
"No, I'm not."
"That's it. I am coming over to see it for myself."
Alex climbs over the handrail and jumps over to Alice's balcony. His right foot slips, and he manages to grab the handrail with his left hand, dropping the champagne glass from his right hand.
"Oh my god!"
Beatrice helps him climb over to her balcony safely.
"You really are mental! You could have fallen."
"Well, I imagine it will have been my last headache."
Alex smiles.
"Don't joke about that."
Beatrice slaps him over the shoulder.
"Now, let's see those beautiful eyes of yours."
Alex grabs her by the waist and pulls her closer to him while gazing into her eyes.
"Tell me a poem."
Beatrice whispers.
"Hmm, I will create one right now inspired by your beauty…"

Beauty

There is beauty in sin.
See the beauty within
There is beauty in death.
Beauty in every breath
Beauty in every season
Life without a reason
Make beauty your prison.

Alex leans over to kiss Beatrice but stops at the last second, just a few millimetres from her lips. He holds on to that moment, keeping her in suspense. Beatrice can't wait any longer, and she kisses him with a burning desire. Both, lost in this moment of deep passion, unconsciously enter Beatrice's room. Alex lifts her up and then gently places her down on the bed. They carry on kissing, touching, and undressing each other slowly. They start making love to each other, missionary positioning Alex on top with slow, deep, and powerful thrusts, wanting to possess her complete body and soul. She feels deeply; every touch, every thrust, every movement gives her a tingly sensation all over her body. Alex holds her hands, their fingers tightly locked together. He lifts her arms above her head and pins her down. He looks her deep in her eyes and whispers.

"You are mine now, all mine."

"Yes, I am yours."

She whispers back to him. They both climax at the same time. Beatrice closes her eyes, letting herself go completely, while Alex removes one of her rings and hides it under the pillow without her noticing.

◆ ◆ ◆

The next morning, Alex dresses up and tries to sneak out before Beatrice awakes. He gently opens the balcony door and takes one step out when he feels an arm on his shoulder. He turns around and sees Beatrice standing there using the bed sheets to cover herself; she has no makeup on, her hair is messy, and her blue eyes sparkling like stars in the night. Alex is caught off guard, completely mesmerized by this "morning angel." So many thoughts are going through his mind: "Why am I running away from this beautiful Angel? What's wrong with me? Why am I running away from love?"

"You were planning to sneak out, I see."
Beatrice smiles gently.
"Well, you did mention something about an early morning."
"So, last night didn't mean anything to you?"
"It did more than I thought it would."
"You say that, but you were sneaking out."
"I don't want to, but I have to. Here, this belongs to you."
Alex takes out of his pocket the ring he stole from her during the night and gives it back.
"What?! You stole my ring."
Beatrice takes a step back.

"I wasn't sure that I managed to steal your heart, so I took your ring to have something to remind me of you."

"I don't know if I should be flattered or upset right now."

"Maybe this will help you decide."

Alex grabs her by the waist, pulls her close, and gives her a passionate kiss, pouring his very soul into it.

◆ ◆ ◆

Jimmy, one of Larry Gold's thugs, impatiently waits in his car, constantly checking the time. Dave opens the car door and jumps in, wearing a navy-striped business suit and a pink shirt and tie.

"What the fuck is this?"

Jimmy looks Dave up and down.

"What?" Dave lifts his shoulders.

"What are you wearing, mate?"

"It's a business suit."

Dave straightens his tie in the mirror.

"I can see that my question was, why are you wearing a suit, Dave?"

"I was thinking about it last night, and you know how the governor always says he's a businessman. So, I decided to dress like one."

"The governor can say whatever the fuck he wants to, but we are gangsters, Dave."

"I know that, Jimmy, but gangsters wear suits, don't they, like in the movies?"

"This ain't a fucking movie, mate, and what's with the pink?"
"What, a lot of businessmen wear pink."
"We are not businessmen, for fuck sakes!"
"Well, we solve problems, right? Businessmen have problems, don't they?"
"Yeah, they call a solicitor when they do."
"Well, sometimes a solicitor is not enough."
"Yes, and they call people like you and me, Dave, fucking gangsters!"
"My point exactly."
"You are stepping on my last nerves, Dave."
"Oh, shit, I forgot my brolly!"
"Who are you, Marry Poppins?"
"A gentleman always carries a brolly."
"So, what now, you are a gentleman?"
"I'm all three: a gentleman, a businessman, and a gangster."
"Forget the brolly; you don't need one."
Jimmy starts the car.
"Patience, Jimmy."
Dave jumps out of the car.
"Dave! Dave!"
Jimmy shouting and blowing the horn.
"Dave!!!!"

◆ ◆ ◆

Jimmy and Dave pull up at Maple Court in Chadwell Heat

at Alex's flat building. They go up the stairs and knock on his door. Alex opens the door wearing a black suit, white shirt, and no tie.

"Who are you?"

Alex opens the door with a surprised look on his face.

"You don't remember us. That hurts my feelings after all the fun we had at the casino."

Jimmy pushes the door wide open.

"Oh yeah, you are one of the gangsters from Stratford."

"We are actually businessmen."

Dave straightens his tie.

"Shut up, Dave. Listen, you are coming with us, alright?"

"No, I'm not."

Alex takes a step back.

"Yeah, you are."

Jimmy takes a step forward.

"Says who?"

"I fucking say so, alright, me Jimmy, Jimmy the Cricket says so."

"Jimmy the Cricket, what is that? Is it your alias? Why do they call you that?"

"Because I make problems go away, and after I'm done, all you hear is crickets."

"I thought it was because you used a cricket bat."

Dave joins the conversation.

"That also, but is not really the fucking point right now, is it?"

"And you, what's your nickname, Mr. Pink?"

Alex looks Dave up and down.

"I can see you might think that, but no, I'm Dave."

"Just Dave?"

"Yeah, it's weird now that you mention it. How come I don't have a nick name? Everyone has one. The governor is Larry Gold; Jimmy and all the other lads have one. I should have one too... I know how about Swinger Dave because I like to swing at people's mugs."

"That's a pornstar name, mate."

"Nah, really?"

"A bit, yeah."

Alex smiles.

"You can't just pick one."

Jimmy turns toward Dave.

"Why not?"

"Because you have to earn it."

"Well, I disagree."

"Fine, then how about Silent Dave?"

"Oh, I like that. It sounds menacing, as if silencing people up."

"No, Silent Dave, as in shut the fuck up Dave! Now grab this bloke, and let's go."

Dave grabs Alex by the arm using his left hand while carrying his brolly in his right hand.

"What are you doing, Dave?"

Jimmy stops Dave by putting his hand on his chest.

"What?"

Dave raises his shoulders.

"You look like you are going on a date. Grab him properly by the collar."

Jimmy grabs Alex by the collar of his shirt.

"Like this, Dave."

"I prefer it my way."

Dave pulls Alex towards him.

"Do it the right way."
Jimmy pulls Alex towards him.
"I got it. Let go."
"No, you don't."
"You let go."
"No, you!"
"No, you!"
Jimmy and Dave start tugging on Alex left and right.
"Fellas, there is no need for this."
Alex is trying to break free. Jimmy pulls harder and tears Alex's shirt.
"Oh, come on, man!"
Alex takes a deep breath.
"I told you I got it."
Dave pulls Alex to his side.
"Ah, shut up, Dave."
Jimmy throws away the piece of fabric stuck between his fingers.
"Fellas, can I go and change?"
"No!"
Dave and Jimmy reply in one voice.

◆ ◆ ◆

Jimmy and Dave are dragging Alex down the stairs into a dark basement. A man is tied down to a chair surrounded by thugs while Larry Gold is punching him in the face with a brass knuckle. The beat-up man sits in a puddle of urine and blood, half dead with a broken jaw, moaning as he is unable to scream anymore. As they reach downstairs, Jimmy turns toward Alex.

"Wait here."

Jimmy goes over to Larry and whispers something in his ear. Larry takes the brass knuckle and hands it to one of his thugs.

"Take this and carry on."

The thug continues beating the poor man. Larry and Jimmy come over to Alex. Larry stops just a few inches from Alex and looks him dead in the eyes.

"Well, well, if it isn't our friend, The Royal Flush."

"Look, man, I mean, sir, whatever I did to offend you, I want you to know I am sorry."

"Is that so?"

Larry takes out his handkerchief from his jacket pocket and wipes off the blood from his hands.

"Yes, I'm really sorry about everything, you know; we were just playing cards. I didn't mean what I said."

Alex is shaking in his shoes.

"What about flirting with my wife?"

"That's, that wasn't me. I was drunk, you know."

Larry starts laughing.

"If I start cracking heads whenever someone flirts with my wife, I would be busy all day, son. That's not why I brought you here."

"Then, why?"

"Do you remember what I told you when I introduced myself?"

"You said you were a ga…"

"Think before you answer."

Larry threatens him by lifting his index finger.

"You said you were a businessman."

"Correct, and as a businessman, I have a

proposition for you, a business opportunity, if you will."

"What?"

"There is a big poker game coming up in Stratford in a couple of days. And since you are more than qualified for this activity, you will play on my behalf, win the game, and I will take home the jackpot."

"Why would I do that? What's in it for me?"

"Good question; this is your incentive."

Larry takes the ruby necklace Alex stole from the Russian wife out of his pocket.

"This exquisite jewellery has a retail value of £15,000, and its sentimental value is undetermined."

Larry dangles the jewellery in front of Alex.

"Where did you get that? It was you; you bought it."

"As I said, this is a great opportunity, which is what they call a win-win situation."

"How is that a win for me? You get all the money; the Russian gets his stupid necklace back. What do I get?"

"Well, the bible does say, "Thou shalt not steal."

"Really, you're going to lecture me about stealing like you never stole anything."

"Of course I did; stealing is good business. All around us, even in nature, animals steal from each other. Stealing is what helped us evolve as a species. From primordial times to ancient Rome all the way to our modern times, people have been stealing, and with God's help, all the way into the future. For as long as humanity and life exist, we shall steal. Stealing solves problems, and getting caught causes problems; that's where you messed up, sonny boy. You are in a pickle right now, as Shakespeare said: "To be or not to be." The game starts on Saturday at 2 pm. Do yourself a favour and be there."

◆ ◆ ◆

Alex returns home to find two men waiting for him inside his flat. One is sitting on his sofa; he is 40 years old with salt and pepper hair, wearing a leather jacket and jeans. The other is browsing through his refrigerator; he is 30 years old, wearing a bomber jacket, an Arsenal t-shirt, and joggers. Alex stops in the doorway.

"Who are you? What are you doing in my home?"

The man sitting on the sofa gets up.

"Relax, we just want to talk to you. I'm Jason, and this is Steve. We are from MI5."

"What the hell is MI5?"

"British intelligence."

Jason takes out his ID badge and shows it to Alex.

"Come on, sit down."

Jason points at the sofa.

"Thanks, I'd rather stand. Don't you need a warrant to get inside my house?"

"Not really, mate, we are not the police."

Steve sticks his head out of the refrigerator.

"There is nothing to eat here."
Steve closes the refrigerator.
"Well, I didn't know you were coming so…"
"If you knew we were coming, that would mean we were bad at what we do."
Jason sits back down on the sofa.
"Can someone please explain to me what's going on?"
"Very well then, you have been recently in contact with a member of the British Royalty."
Jason puts his feet up on the coffee table.
"No, I haven't."
"I guess she was just another bird for you, right?"
Steve steps closer to Alex.
"What?!"
Alex raises his eyebrows.
"The name Beatrice rings a bell."
Jason crosses his arms around his chest.
"Well, yeah, wait, you're saying she is a…"
"She is the future Duchess of Essex, but you already knew that, right?"
Steve gets into Alex's face.
"You were also in contact with a Russian Oligarch; care to share with us what you discussed."
"Nothing important, just the weather, his babushka…"
"His babushka."
Jason takes his feet down from the coffee table.
"I suggest we take him to interrogation right away. I guarantee I can make this bird sing."
Steve grabs Alex.
"Your input has been noted; now stand down."
Steve lets go of Alex and takes a few steps back.

"I apologise if my colleague made you feel uncomfortable."
Jason gets up and walks over to Alex.
"You shouldn't worry about him. It's me you should worry about. Your record may be clean, but you are on my naughty list. If you are indeed a spy or carry essential information and refuse to share it with us, I will make your life a living hell; you can bet on that. Do I make myself clear?"
"Yes," Alex whispers.
"Don't be shy now; give us a bell."
Jason sticks a phone number into Alex's pocket and heads out the door, followed by Steve.
"Cheer up, mate. You have two guardian angels now."
Steve smiles while passing Alex on his way out.

❖ ❖ ❖

Alex walks slowly on Southend Pier early in the morning at sunrise. The pier is the world's longest, and it stretches for 1.33 miles out into the sea. It is made from metal pillars and wooded boards. It also has a train track, a small train carrying tourists back and forth. Alex reaches the end, climbs over the handrail, and stands on the edge, looking down at the sea as the weaves are crashing into the pillars. As the sun appears over the horizon, light rays hit Alex in the face. Suddenly, the sun acts as a torch flashing Alex, and an unknown voice whispers his name.

"Alex."

Alex loses his balance and manages to grab hold of the handrail, which stops him from falling into the sea. He panics for a moment, trying to get a foothold, and barely manages to climb back up over the handrail and back to safety on the pier. He falls on his ass.

"What the hell is going on? I was about to jump."

The wind stops blowing, and he can hear an unknown voice calling his name louder and louder.

"Alex, Alex."

He panics, gets up, and starts running back to shore. He can hear his heartbeat louder and louder, the unknown voice calling his name again.

"Alex, Alex."

Fear grabs hold of him as he desperately tries to run away from that voice.

"Butterfly, butterfly!"

Alex starts shouting from the top of his lungs.

"Butterfly, butterfly!"

In the blink of an eye, Alex is back in his flat, sitting on the sofa. He jumps up.

"How did I get back home? Was it a dream? What the hell is going on?"

He goes and looks inside the refrigerator.

"There is nothing to drink in this house."

Alex leaves the flat, goes up the street, passes Chadwell Heath train station, and goes down the road to the old Eva Hart Pub. The Pub was named after a local resident, Eva Hart, who was a Titanic survivor. You can find pictures of Eva Hart and her family on the walls inside the pub and other important figures who visited Eva Hart or were involved in the development of the Chadwell Heath community. Alex goes to the bar and orders a pint of beer. As he turns around, he accidentally bumps into a group of three young men and spills his beer on himself.

"Careful, mate."

"Watch it."

"Sorry, fellas."

Alex apologises while trying to wipe off his jeans. One of the three men pushes him.

"Hey, leave the guy alone. You should pay attention to where you're going."

The bartender takes Alex's side.

"Now, behave yourself, or I will throw you out."

"It's calm, no harm done. Let's go, boys."

The three men go up the stairs to the upper level.

"What a bunch of twats. Don't worry about that. Let me get you another one."

The bartender goes to pour another pint.

"I think I need something stronger than that."

"What will it be?"

"A Jack and Coke, please."

"Jack and Coke coming right up."

Alex drinks it all in one shot.

"Cheers, where is the toilet?"

"Up the stairs and to the right."

"Thanks."

Alex goes up the stairs at a slow and heavy pace. He goes inside and cleans his trousers. As he is about to exit, the three men from early are entering the toilet.

"Well, look who we have here."

"Are you all right, mate?"

"Fellas, I'm not looking for trouble."

Alex takes a step back.

"We are not looking for trouble. Also, it's a bit rude of you to assume that, don't you think?"

"No, that's not what I meant."

"I agree with my mate that's rude."

"We can't have that; rude people are not welcome in our pub."

"Fellas, please.."

One of the three men punches Alex in his abdomen. Alex runs and hides in one of the toilet stalls, closing the door behind him. The men start knocking at the door.

"You're all right in there, mate?"

"You don't look too good."

"You should come out and get some fresh air."

Alex sits on the toilet heavily, breathing, and starts talking to himself.

"I need to fight; I want to teach these cunts a lesson. I need a UFC fighter... I got it, ten, nine, eight...one."

Alex opens the door and kicks one of them in the chest so hard he sends him flying into the wall. Alex then proceeds to punch a second one repeatedly into the face. The third man attacks Alex from behind, punching and kicking him with little effect whatsoever. Alex is completely unfazed and focused on the guy in front of him. He continues to punch him until his target falls to the ground, completely unconscious. Alex then turns his attention to the sneaky guy who attacked him from behind. He takes him down and grabs him in an armbar and breaks his arm, then he grabs one of his legs and, with a swift move, breaks his ankle. The man who got kicked in the chest recovers and attacks Alex, who gets back on his feet. From three against one, now is just the two of them. Alex has rendered one of his attackers unconscious and the other one down on the floor in complete agony with a broken arm and leg. Alex takes a few steps back, moving the fight to the centre of the room. Alex and his opponent can see their reflections in the mirror. They both take a boxing stance and start throwing blows at each other. His opponent is twice his size, but Alex has no problem holding his own. Both are getting injured, blood pouring over their face as they continue brutally hitting each other. Alex gets down low, launches at his opponent, grabs him by the waist, and then throws him down on the floor. After that, he gets on top and ferociously punches down on his opponent, who struggles to protect himself. His opponent loses consciousness, lying there on the floor in a pool of his own blood. Alex gets up and looks down at his prey.

"I butchered your face; look at you! Curled up like a bitch!"

Alex is banging on his chest.

"Do something, come on, do something!"

Alex catches a glimpse of himself in the mirror, and he sees a killer with a bloody face and knuckles. This beast looking back at him makes him tremble with fear.

"No, no! What have I done? Butterfly, butterfly!"

◆ ◆ ◆

Beatrice and her parents, Edward and Catarina, the Duke and Duchess of Essex, sit at a fancy riverside restaurant in Richmond. Alex comes over in a rush.

"Hi, I'm sorry I'm late."

"Hi."

Beatrice gets up and tries to kiss Alex, but he turns away and hugs her instead.

"It's not a big deal that you are only half an hour late."

"Dad."

Beatrice gives her dad a condescending look.

"Let me introduce you to my parents: my mom, Catarina, and my dad, Edward, the third Duke of Essex."

Alex reaches out for a handshake, then stops.

"I'm sorry, but I have never met any royals. Is this okay? Am I allowed to shake your hand, or what's the custom?"

The duke gets up from his chair.

"It's perfectly fine. Please call me, Edward. Have a seat, young man."

The duke points at an empty chair after shaking Alex's hand.

"Nice to meet you, sir, ma'am."

"The pleasure is all ours, and you don't have to be

so formal."
The duchess smiles at Alex.
"The waiter comes along to take Alex's order."
"Good day, sir. May I take your order?"
"Yes, he will have a scotch, the same as I will."
The duke points at his glass.
"No, I shouldn't. I'm driving."
"It's one drink, and there is no harm in that."
"I suppose."
"Do you care for some ice, sir?"
"What part of the same as mine didn't you understand?"
"My apologies, sir."
The waiter leaves while the duchess and Beatrice stare at the duke with judgmental eyes.
"That was a bit excessive."
The duchess rolls her eyes.
"You know how much I hate having to repeat myself. Was I not clear enough?"
The duke takes a sip of scotch. The waiter brings over Alex's drink.
"Enjoy your drink, sir," says the waiter as he hurriedly left.
"He left without asking if we needed anything else. That's a bit rude, isn't it?"
"Who is rude, you or him?"
Beatrice plays with her hair.
"How am I being rude for pointing out the fact that he is not doing his job properly? Am I right, Alex?"
"Well, maybe."
"See, Alex gets it."
"Okay, enough about the waiter. I'm more interested in Alex at the moment. Why don't you

tell us a bit about yourself? What do you do for work?"

The duchess turns toward Alex.

"I'm an Uber driver and…"

"Well, that is something, I guess."

"Dad."

"What? I have nothing against the working class, and surely a man can do better than that."

"Well, he is also a poet who writes poetry."

"A poet taxi driver is something, all right."

"Dad!"

"What? I meant it."

"That sounds lovely; why don't you tell us one of your poems, Alex?"

The duchess takes a sip of champagne.

"I'm sorry, I don't feel particularly romantic right now."

"That's a shame. Then again, a brilliant poet should be able to come up with something on the spot."

The duke gives Alex a condescending look.

"I have one for you since we discussed my job."

"Lovely, let's hear it."

My Job

> My Job, my job
> When did you
> Become my God?
> Keeping me up
> Late at night.
> Waking me up
> Before daylight.
> Deciding for me
> When to eat,
> When to sleep.
> Stealing my time
> Controlling my life.

"That was a lovely poem."
The duchess softly claps her hands.
"I suppose so."
"Dad!"
"All I'm saying is that poetry is not an essential skill, such as hunting. Have you ever been hunting Alex?"
"No, I haven't."
"Of course not. Anyway, you should try it. Nothing in the world compares to the rush you feel from stalking prey. I could tell you so many stories from

my trips to Africa."

"Dad, no."

"What? I haven't been there in ten years, thanks to you."

"I don't want you killing innocent animals."

"Innocent animals?"

The duke gives Beatrice a condescending look.

"Dad, please."

"Women, what can I say? They will always find a way to put an end to whatever gives a man pleasure. Fine, there will be no more hunting discussions on the condition that you two girls go and powder your nose so I can have a conversation with Alex from hunter to pacifist."

"Dad, you promised to be nice."

"My sweet Beatrice, you worry too much. When did I ever break a promise? Now give us a kiss and fly away, my hummingbird."

Beatrice and the duchess leave the table.

"It's just you and me now, soft boy. The first thing I want you to know…"

"I think I know what you want to say. Please let me start first."

"That was a bit rude, cutting me off, but fine, you have my permission; after all, I promised to be nice."

"I really like your daughter; actually, it is more than that; I love her. I haven't told anyone this, not even her, but I fell in love the moment I saw her. She is more than I could ever ask for, more than I deserve, that's for sure. She really is the love of my life, the woman of my dreams. And if you can give me one chance, I promise I will spend my life doing everything I can to make her happy."

A moment of silence.

"Well, that's a shame because I need you to break

up with her."
"Why?"
"It's like you said, she is great, there for she should marry someone from a good family. It's nothing personal; you seem to be a great lad, but unfortunately, you were born into the wrong family. She will marry someone worthy of her status, and surely you can understand that."
"No, I don't."
"Don't make this harder on yourself and break up with her before this little summer romance escalates any further."
"Why don't you do it then? Why don't you tell her not to see me again?"
"Well, she seems to fancy you also. Besides, what kind of father do you think I am? I'm not going to break my daughter's heart. No, no, you will do it."
"And if I refuse?"
"Well then, I suppose I will have to go hunting again."
The Duchess and Beatrice return to the table.
"Perfect timing, girls."
"Should we order something to eat?"
The duchess asks her husband.
"We should, but we are still waiting for Alex to finish his drink. Is the scotch too strong for you?"
Alex knocks it down in one heartbeat.
"Compared to Romanian palinca, your scotch is extremely weak."
"Well, in that case, I suggest you try the veal. It looks a bit ruff on the outside, but it's very tender..."

◆ ◆ ◆

Alex walks inside Asper Casino in Stratford, escorted by Larry Gold and his thugs. Alex and Larry are walking side by side in front of the group. Larry gives him another lecture.

"Listen, son, I know you don't like me that much. Who loves his boss, right? I, for one, like that; I don't want love. I don't need people to love me, and I don't need love from anyone, not even from my wife. I need them to fear me, and when people fear you, they will never consider disrespecting you. You see, fear is the glue that holds society together; fear keeps the sheep in line—fear of authority, fear of getting caught, fear of God's judgment. You see, God knows the importance of fear. He, in His infinite wisdom, created Hell to keep the people in line and obey the Ten Commandments. If you stop and think about it, I follow His steps. After all, we are made in His image, are we not? Not only that but at a more personal level, I hate love. To me, love feels like begging, and I don't beg."

All this time, Alex is distracted and nervous, constantly looking the other way. Larry eventually notices that Alex is not paying attention.

"Hey, are you paying attention to what I'm saying here?"

Larry snaps his fingers while Alex keeps walking without answering.

"Mate, wake up!"

Jimmy puts his hand on Alex's shoulder and shakes him a bit.

"Sorry, what?"

Alex looks back at Larry.

"What's wrong with you? Get your mind in the game. Do us a favour and use those psychology tricks of yours to win this, all right?"

"Yeah, sure, I just need to go to the toilet."

"Fine, Jimmy, go with him."

Larry snaps his fingers. Alex goes and locks himself in a toilet stall.

"Hey, why are you locking the door?"

Jimmy knocks on the door.

"What, do you want to see me taking a shit?"

Alex shouts from behind the door.

"Just hurry up, mate."

Alex sits on the toilet, talking out loud.

"This is getting out of hand. I have to stop doing this count down… But if I stop, then I will lose her. She will never love me, the real me. I have no choice, even though I don't have the confidence or the courage to keep going. But I know someone who does… Ten, nine, eight…one."

Alex comes out of the toilet filled with confidence and takes his place at the poker table.

"Good luck to everyone; you're going to need it."

Alex smiles and winks.

◆ ◆ ◆

As time goes by, Alex moves to the final after

systematically taking out all his opponents individually. At the final table is Alex, a brunette woman covered in tattoos, an old man, a man dressed all in black with sunglasses, and a nerd. The game starts slow, with each player observing each other, waiting for the right moment to raise the game. Alex plays with his chips, watching everybody like a hawk. The man dressed in black starts a conversation with the brunette girl with tattoos.

"I hate this part when everything goes slow."
"Yeah, me too; this is boring."
"I agree, care to make it interesting."
The man in black takes down his sunglasses.
"What do you have in mind?"
"How about we have a little wager for ourselves?"
"Name your price."
The brunette girl smiles back at him.
"Not money that is boring."
"What then?"
"Well, since you love tattoos, if I win, you get a heart tattoo on your sexy ass with my name on it."
"That's a bit much, isn't it?"
"Fine, just use my initials instead; it will be our little secret."
"Ok, and if I win?"
"Name your price?"
The man in black smiles back at her.
"You don't have any tattoos, do you?"
"No, and I don't like where this is going."
"Relax, you don't have to get my name tattooed."
"What?"
"Something more personal, inspiring, and beautiful, like a butterfly on your lower back."
Alex drops his chips from his hand instantly and starts shaking.
"No, not that. See, even this guy doesn't like it."

The man in black points at Alex.
"Yeah, you will get a butterfly."
"No, not a butterfly, come on."
"A pink butterfly."
"Can you stop saying butterfly?"
Alex snaps back at them.
"Oh, I think we found your kryptonite."
The man dressed in black smiles at Alex.
"I don't have any weakness. I will raise you £200."
Alex throws a few chips into the pot.
"It's not your turn, sir."
The dealer gives Alex his chips back.
"Oh, I like my odds; here's your £200."
The man in black starts laughing.
"Sir, it is not permitted to taunt other players."
"Apologies."
The man in black leans back in his chair.
"Sir, it is your turn now."
The dealer points at Alex.
"Call you and raise another £200."
Alex adds chips to the pot. The other three players fold, and only Alex and the man in black are left playing this hand.
"Let's skip the boring part, shall we? I'm all in."
The man in black adds all his chips to the pot.
"Check, all in."
Alex shakes while adding his chips to the pot.
"You don't seem too sure about yourself."
The man in black smiles.
"Don't worry about me. I'm fine."
Alex starts biting his nails.
"Oh, I'm not worried at all."
The dealer reveals the fifth card, the river, leaving Alex in complete shock as he loses.
"Better luck next time, buddy."
The man in black collects all the chips. Alex takes a

deep breath and then attacks the dealer.

"You did this; you gave me the wrong cards. You played me. You two are working together. You son of a bitch!"

Security escorts Alex outside the casino.

◆ ◆ ◆

A busy afternoon in London, Alex stands outside Whitechapel train station, looking straight ahead with empty eyes as people cross his path. He starts counting down out loud, and people avoid him or ignore him like he is a madman.

"Ten, nine, eight, seven, six, five, four, three, two, one."

Alex takes a deep breath, and then he starts throwing punches left and right. He knocks down the first two people crossing his path as they are caught completely off guard. After that, most people run away, trying to escape Alex's uncontrollable rage. People take cover inside some stores, and others cross the road in a mad panic and get hit by passing cars. People run and scream while the unsuspected drivers shout back at the pedestrians. Alex creates chaos while people desperately shout.

"Help, please help!"
"Hey, watch out!"
"Someone call the police!"

Alex continues to assault people left and right while laughing. He is completely out of control, but he loves every moment. The sound of a police car approaching gives people hope; however, they are stuck in traffic. People desperately begging the police officers for help.

"Help, help! Come quick; he is crazy."
"Help, he is attacking people on the street."

The two police officers abandon their car and are chasing Alex on foot. Alex sees the police, but instead of running away from them, he starts taunting them and continues to laugh, enjoying himself more and more. Alex starts running a circle around a car while the police officers chase him. He then knocks over a cyclist, takes his bike, and throws it through an office building window. He then jumps inside and assaults the people working there. Alex starts throwing computers left and right and destroying furniture while the people inside are running for their lives towards the nearest exit, some of them jumping out on the street through the broken window. The two police officers enter the building through the broken window. A few moments pass, and Alex jumps out the window. He manages to escape from the two police officers. He takes a moment to look around and spots the abandoned police car. Alex jumps behind the wheel and speeds away, damaging other cars. Two police cars appear out of nowhere and immediately start pursuing Alex. The police chase causes more chaos throughout London.

More and more police cars join in the pursuit. Alex eventually ends up on Westminster Bridge, where a police force blockade is waiting for him. Halfway up the bridge, Alex makes a hard turn left and crashes into the side of the bridge. Alex steps out of the car with a bloody face, feeling a bit dizzy and stumbling. He takes a deep breath as police officers surround him at gunpoint. Alex takes a step back and leans on the concrete edge.

"Wow, this was the best GTA game ever. It was so real."

Alex wipes off the blood from his face.

"Get down right now!"

"Down on your knees!"

"Get down!" A police officer shouts at Alex.

"Wait a minute, why are we in London? GTA is in LA, not in London. Wait, is this real?"

"Get down; this is your final warning!"

"Get down now!"

Alex looks back over his shoulder down at Thames River and then back at the police.

"Fuck it, it's the only way."

Alex jumps over the edge into the river while shouting.

"Butterfly!!!"

◆ ◆ ◆

Alex, in handcuffs and chains around his waist and ankles, is escorted into an empty courtroom by two special police officers. They place him into a safety box designed for dangerous criminals. One of the police officers breaks the silence.

"Hey, sit down." Alex nervously obeys.

A few moments go by, and then the judge, the prosecutor, and the stenographer walk in. The judge is 60 years old with white hair and a severe expression on his face. The prosecutor is 35 years old; he is tall, has dark hair, and has a bored expression on his face. As the judge walks in, the police officer whispers to Alex.

"Hey, stand up."

Alex gets up, and when the judge sits down, Alex also sits down.

"Hey, stand up!"

"What?"

Alex replies, confused.

"I told you to stand up."

"Why? Everyone is sitting down, so why can't I?"

"Because you are the accused, you don't get to sit down while the judge is in session."

"Fine."

Alex stands back up. The judge looks left and right

at the prosecutor and the stenographer.
"Where is his lawyer?"
"I don't know, maybe he's late."
The prosecutor answers while looking over some documents.
"Great, can someone go look for him?"
"I will send one of the officers from the hallway to search for him."
The prosecutor steps outside for a moment and then returns to his desk. A few moments later, a police officer enters the courtroom.
"Sorry, your honour, we couldn't find him."
"Thanks, keep an eye out for him anyway."
"Will do, your honour."
The police officer leaves the room.
"I will give him ten more minutes if he doesn't show up. I will have no choice but to cancel today's hearing and issue a fine to the lawyer for not fulfilling his legal responsibilities."
"That seems about right."
The prosecutor puts his documents in order.
"In the meantime, let's go out for a cigarette, shall we?"
"I can't say no to that."
The judge and prosecutor exit the room.
"Hey, sit down. The judge is no longer present in the room."
The police officer knocks on the table.
"Why, what's the point? When he comes back, I will have to stand up again." Alex replies irritated.
"Yes, you will stand up again, but in the meantime, sit down."
"Yeah, but it doesn't make sense."
"Don't make me come in there with you. If I tell you to sit down, you sit down. If I tell you to stand, you will stand. Got it!"

"Okay, okay."

Alex takes a seat. A few moments later, the judge and prosecutor return. Alex stands back up before the police officer has a chance to say anything.

"Still missing, I guess I have no choice but to..."

Before the judge finishes his sentence, Alex's lawyer rushes inside the courtroom, sweating and breathing heavily.

"You are late, and you were scheduled for a court hearing today at 2 pm; you are half an hour late."

"Your honour, I am deeply sorry, but.."

"I'm not done. Don't interrupt me; your lack of time management is disrespectful toward the court and your client, whose future hangs in the balance. Since your client is a first-time offender, I will pardon you today, but any future disrespect will not be tolerated. Do I make myself clear?"

"Crystal clear, your honour, thank you."

"Very well, then, prosecutor, please proceed."

The hearing ends in minutes, leaving Alex totally confused by all the legal terminology. The only thing he understood was: "The accused will remain in custody until trial." The judge slams down his gavel and then exits the courtroom. One by one, everyone else leaves. Alex's lawyer rushes out without saying a word to Alex or even looking at him. The stenographer approaches Alex and hands him a piece of paper to sign. Alex looks left and right, not knowing what to do. His heartbeat rises as he starts to panic.

"Sign it, and let's go."

The police officer points at the bottom of the page. Alex signs it with a shaking hand when suddenly the light starts to flicker, and an unknown voice whispers his name.

"Alex."

Suddenly, Alex finds himself in the middle of a raging

river on a small piece of land. The small island splits the river in two. On the left side, the water is dirty and dark brown, and on the right side, the water is clean and crystal clear. Alex can see the rocks at the bottom of the river. He takes a deep breath and jumps over to the right bank of the river over the clear water. Alex then starts walking through a forest while the sun is setting down, casting shadows. Feeling that something isn't right, fear creeps down his spine. All of a sudden, a group of people emerges from behind the threes, and they surround him. Alex is unable to speak or move as panic sets in. When a woman takes a step towards Alex, looks him dead in the eyes and says: "You will never leave this place."

◆ ◆ ◆

LIMBO

Alex sits on his living room sofa, staring at the ceiling. He takes a deep breath and then jumps up, knocking over the coffee table.

"What the fuck is going on! What do you mean I will never leave this place?"

Alex paces nervously back and forth in his living room, saying the same thing repeatedly.

"You will never leave this place; you will never leave this place."

A knock on his door. He opens it and sees Jimmy and Dave outside his flat. Jimmy punches Alex in his stomach.

"This is for running away after the game."

Alex catches his breath. Dave and Jimmy grab him and start dragging him down the stairs.

"Boss wants to have a word with you."

Dave plays with his umbrella while walking down the stairs. Alex takes a deep breath and starts a countdown.

"Ten, nine, eight.."

"What the fuck is he doing?"

Dave and Jimmy look at each other.

"I think he is counting the stairs."
"Who the fuck does that, Dave?"
"I don't know, Jimmy. I'm just saying."
"Seven, six, five, four."
Alex continues counting.
"Yeah, you are right. This is weird."
"Do you remember he went mad after losing the game?"
"I don't know, Dave, maybe. He did jump on the dealer."
"Three, two, one."
Reaching the ground floor, Alex snatches the umbrella from Dave and then beats them both using some kung fu moves. The fight ends in seconds, leaving Dave and Jimmy lying on the ground in pain and agony. Alex walks out of the building, taking Dave's umbrella.
"Ah fuck, the boss is not going to like this."
Jimmy gets up slowly.
"Yeah, not to mention he took my brolly too."
Dave is still lying down on the ground, attending to his wounds.
"That's what you worry about?"
"Yeah, I did pay £20 quid for it."
"I swear to God, when I get my hands on him, I will shove that fucking brolly up your ass and open it."

◆ ◆ ◆

Alex walks inside The Savoy using the umbrella as a walking cane and goes straight to the reception.
"Hi, is my room ready?"
"Yes, sir, as requested, we have sent a bottle of champagne to your room."
"Thanks."
"If you need anything else, please let us know."
"Will do."
Alex takes the elevator up to room 108, goes inside, drops the umbrella on the floor, and pours himself a glass of champagne. Then he hears a soft knock on his door. He opens it and sees a gorgeous redhead woman wearing a black leather skirt and boots with a leopard top. The gorgeous redhead is none other than Larry Gold's wife. Alex looks her up and down.
"You are late."
"Well, good things deserve the..."
"Come in and shut the door."
Alex turns his back on her and goes back into the room. She pauses for a moment, surprised by Alex's rude behaviour, but she nevertheless follows him inside. Alex leans back against the wall, sipping his champagne.
"I could use a drink."
"The bottle is over there; help yourself."
Alex points at the champagne bottle.
"A gentleman will have poured a drink for me too."
She pours a glass for herself, then turns around, looking back at Alex with fire in her eyes.
"I never claimed to be a gentleman."

Alex starts an eye-starting contest with her determined not to lose whatever the cost.
"You know my husband is looking for you all over London."
"I know."
Alex, unfazed, takes a sip of champagne.
"I wonder what will happen if he finds us here."
"There will be blood."
"Yours or his?"
"Call him and find out."
"So, you are some sort of gangster?"
"No, I'm not."
"What then?"
"I am the beast."
"The beast?"
"Yeah, the beast."
Alex recites The Beast poem.

The Beast

My temper animalistic

Driven by instinct.

Feeding on passion

Devoted to sin.

Ready to devour,

Every day, every hour

The blood in your veins

Live and die in vain.

In an instant, Alex throws his glass down on the floor and launches at her, knocks her champagne glass from her hand, grabs her by the neck, and pins her down against the wall. His fingers squeeze her neck so that she can barely breathe. Alex gives her a powerful, passionate kiss and then bites her lower lip so hard that it starts to bleed. After that, Alex rips open her top and bends her over the table, knocking down the champagne bottle and splashing champagne over her face and breasts. Alex takes out his belt and ties her hands behind her back.

"I'm going to fuck you so bad right now. Spread your legs!"

She obeys him and spreads her legs.

"Yeah, just like that, you fucking slut!"

Alex leans forward and whispers in her ear.

"I'm going to rape you."

Her entire body shivers and trembles as Alex takes her from behind like a wild beast.

◆ ◆ ◆

An hour later, Dave and Jimmy arrive at The Savoy, and they go up to room 108. Dave stands on the right side of the door, and Jimmy on the left. Jimmy takes out a stunt gun out of his pocket.

"Okay, Dave, you open the door, and I will take care of this cunt."

Dave reaches for the door handle, and Alex throws

Larry's wife out when the door opens.

"Fuck off slut."

Jimmy teases Alex, who falls on the floor, and then Jimmy and Dave proceed to hit him and electrocute him repeatedly.

"You ain't so though now, are you cunt?"

"You fucking tosser!"

◆ ◆ ◆

Jimmy and Dave drag Alex, half dead, all beaten, down into a basement where Larry and his thugs are waiting for them. Larry takes a step closer to Jimmy.

"You are a mess and also late. Care to explain?"

"Sorry, boss, we hit a bit of a snag."

"A snag."

"He pulled off some karate crap and got away the first time."

Dave is attending to his wounds.

"Karate?"

"Yes, boss."

"But you have a gun, Dave, don't you?"

"Yes, boss, but.."

"So, what then is the gun not working?"

"Yes, boss, I think it does."
"Let's have a look, shall we?"
Larry snaps his fingers, and Dave hands over his gun.
"What kind of boss would I be if I didn't give you the proper tools to succeed? It looks fine, but one can never be too sure."
"Bang!"
Larry shoots Dave in the leg.
"Yeah, it works just fine."
Dave falls in agony.
"There is something else, boss."
"Surprises keep on coming, hey Jimmy." shouted Larry
"We tracked him down at The Savoy."
"Our boy here has some expensive taste."
"He was not alone."
"Come on, Jimmy, spill the beans."
"Sorry, boss, he was with your wife."
"So, you're telling me, right, you let him get away so he can shag my wife before bringing him here, is that it?"
"Sorry, boss."
"Congratulations, Jimmy, you are now the employee of the month."
"Sorry, boss."
"I will deal with you later, now fuck off!"
Larry goes to Alex.
"Everyone wants to be the boss, isn't it? See what you have to deal with daily: nothing but incompetence. I hate incompetent people, among many things, and now I will have to add my bitter half to that long list because of you. There is one thing that I love, and that is corporations. The idea of a corporation is the best thing we invented since slavery. You see, slaves were used until they

died, and nothing was given to them, no care or concern, no love, and certainly no hope. And that's the genius idea behind corporations: they give slaves hope. Hope for a better day, hope for a promotion, hope for a raise or Christmas bonus. You see, the masters realized that slaves work even harder when they have hope. And they dangle that carrot in your face until you end up on your back six feet under. "Hallelujah!"

"Please, you don't have to do this. You don't have to be a gangster."

Alex breathes heavily.

"I hate repeating myself!"

Larry hits Alex with the gun.

"If you kill me, you will not get your money back."

"Your Russian friend is knee-deep in brick and mortar, and if I return his precious jewel, I might get my shoes dirty. That takes care of the first part of our problem. The second issue of the day, Dave over there, informed me you have a girlfriend. I will have to pay her a visit so that your debt is paid in full."

"No, not Beatrice. She has nothing to do with this."

"Beatrice, that's a posh name. What do you say, lads, fancy a round with a posh bird?"

"No, no, please!"

"Too late, son. The first rule of business is to get rid of liabilities. I hereby regret to inform you that we have to let you go."

"No, no, please!"

"Looks like you will not rest in peace."

"R.I.P"

"What!?"

Alex recites R.I.P. poem.

R.I.P

Pledging allegiance to war

My heart bleeds peace.

Addicted to violence,

More and more.

Death is my desire,

May I rest in peace,

In the eternal fire.

"That was very poetic and funny. Because I'm about to fire a bullet in your skull."

Larry points the gun at Alex's head. Alex starts a slow

countdown, taking a pause between each number.

"Ten, nine…"

"Is he counting down? You have some big Jacobs on you, son."

"Boss, shoot him now, don't let him finish."

"Zip it, Jimmy. You disappointed me today. "

"Boss, listen to me."

"Are you craving for a bullet too, Jimmy?"

Larry points the gun at Jimmy.

"Eight, seven…"

Alex continues, and the lights start flickering. Alex hears a mechanical clock in the background.

"Tick, tock.."

Larry points the gun back at Alex.

"Six, five, let's count together."

Larry smiles while Alex begins to hear an unknown voice whispering his name.

"Alex, Alex."

"Four, three.."

"Alex, can you hear me?"

The unknown voice grows louder.

"Two.."

Larry cocks back the gun.

"Alex, wake up!"

"One."

"Alex!!!"

Bang!

◆ ◆ ◆

Doctor Kingsley walks inside St George Hospital while talking on the phone with his assistant.

"Hi, doctor. I just wanted to inform you that your last appointment was cancelled."

"Well, in that case, take the rest of the day off."

"Nice."

"Just forward all the calls to my number, and please get some more biscuits for tomorrow, the ones I like."

"Will do that. Are you going to the hospital today?"

"I'm here now, actually."

"Fingers crossed, who knows, maybe today is the day."

"You know me, I never give up."

"That's another way of saying stubborn as a mule."

"Hey, being stubborn is a quality in this case, anyway."

"Good luck, doctor."

"Thanks, bye."

Doctor Kingsley walks inside a patient room where Alex is lying down on the bed, eyes closed, connected to medical machines.

"How many times do I have to tell people to keep this clock close to you?"

Doctor Kingsley moves a clock on the nightstand

closer to Alex.

"Do you feel like waking up today? What do you say?"

The doctor looks down on Alex and then takes a torch out of his pocket.

"You know, studies have shown that a coma patient can respond to sound and might experience even light sensitivity. So, let's shine some light into the darkness, shall we?"

Doctor Kingsley points the torch at Alex's face, focusing on his eyes and turning it on and off while saying his name.

"Alex, Alex, can you hear me? Alex, wake up. Alex!!!"

Alex opens his eyes and jumps up in bed.

"It's okay, you are safe. Alex, try to relax; you are safe now."

Alex breathes heavily.

"Doctor Kingsley, what's going on? Where am I?"

"You are in the hospital, and you are safe."

The on-call doctor and a nurse enter the room.

"Hey, look who's up? How are you doing, buddy?"

"Okay, I guess."

"Let me have a look at you."

The on-call doctor runs some routine checks on Alex.

"All looks okay, not bad, considering you were in a coma for three months."

"A coma?"

"Nothing to be alarmed of; you seem to be fully recovered."

"What's the last thing you remember?"

Doctor Kingsley asked Alex.

"I was shot, he shot me, and that's how I ended up in a coma."

"Nobody shot you. They found you in a coma in

your flat."

"Alex, listen to me; whatever you saw wasn't real. You are safe now."

Doctor Kingsley tries to console Alex.

"No, no, I don't believe you."

"Alex, listen to me, it wasn't real. Whatever you experienced, it was all just a dream."

"No, no, don't say that I don't believe it; it was real, and she is real. I know what I felt; you can't tell me it wasn't real."

"Alex, listen to me."

"Shit, I have to save her. He said he was going after her."

"Sir, you need to calm down."

The on-call doctor puts his hand on Alex's chest.

"No, get away from me, all of you!"

Alex pushes the doctor away and jumps out of bed.

"Call security."

The on-call doctor turns toward the nurse.

"There is no need for that; let me handle this."

Doctor Kingsley tries to calm down the situation.

"No, get away from me; you work for them, all of you!"

"Alex, when was our last session? Do you remember that?"

"He said he was going to make my life a living hell. And you, you worked for them from the start, I know."

"Who do you think I work for? Tell me, Alex?"

"For them, MI5, don't deny it. It's all clear now that you played me from the start, just like I played that old geezer."

"Alex, please listen to me; whatever happened to you, we can talk about it, okay?"

"No, no, I'm not falling for your tricks again. I'm not giving up on her. I have to save her no matter

what"
"Save who?"
"She is all I've ever wanted and the woman of my dreams. Nobody is going to take her away from me, not you, not her snob father, no one."
"What's her name, Alex? Tell me her name."
"Get out of my way!"
Alex pushes Doctor Kingsley aside and runs out of the room, two security guards on his heels.
"No, no, let me handle this."
"Nurse, prepare a syringe. We have to sedate him."
The on-call doctor addresses the nurse.
"It's a bad idea. I know he is in shock, but let's wait for him to calm down naturally."
"This is my hospital. I make the rules here, and he is a danger to himself and my staff. We must stop him before it escalates."
"You risk aggravating his condition, or worse, he may end up back in a coma."
"I have been a medical doctor for over 30 years. I don't need you to question my methods; now step aside, or security will escort you out."
The security guards capture Alex and hold him down while the on-call doctor sedates him.
"Get off, let me go!"
Alex desperately tries to break free.
"I need to reset; I need to reset."
"Alex, look at me. I will be by your side when you wake up, okay? I promise."
Doctor Kingsley tries to comfort Alex.
"Butterfly, butterfly."
Alex repeats the word butterfly over and over as his eyes close.

❖ ❖ ❖

In the St George Hospital psychiatric department in the communal room where patients interact with each other by playing games or watching TV, Alex sits alone in the corner, swaying back and forth while constantly repeating the word butterfly. Doctor Kingsley and the head of the psychiatry department, Doctor Thomas, are having a conversation, looking at Alex from a distance.

"I believe that Alex experimented with self-hypnosis and somehow ended up in a self-induced coma right from the start. Doctor Thomas, what can I say? I blame myself for his condition, myself, and that on-call idiot. I should press charges even if I risk losing my own license to practice."

"Well, there are various factors to consider that led to his condition; however, I must say a self-induced coma is not common."

"I didn't realize the severity of his condition. When I awaken him, I probably turn off a switch in his mind. I pulled the plug into whatever fantasy or movies played in his mind. When I noticed, I tried to get as much information as possible, but that arrogant fool ended it, and now here we are."

"Yes, I agree with you, Doctor Kingsley. Unable to cope with reality, he had a severe shock, and his mind entered into a loop state."

"I think that the word butterfly that he keeps repeating is very important. It might be the key to unlocking this puzzle that his mind created."

"Well, based on the information you provided and my initial tests, I concluded that his mind and body are disconnected. Therefore, we will start a ten-day exposure therapy session. Cold exposure, we will submit him to ice baths. Exposing his body to a cold environment will trigger a response in his brain, hopefully reconnecting his brain and body. We will use his body to pull him out of the fantasy world he constructed and ground him back into reality."

"That would work if I could assist him, as I made a promise to him."

"I could use another sharp mind in the room."

"Okay, thank you for your help, Doctor Thomas."

"Good day, Doctor Kingsley."

"Let me just say goodbye to Alex, and I will be on my way."

Doctor Kingsley walks over to Alex.

"I have failed you, Alex, and I am deeply sorry for that."

"Butterfly, butterfly."

Alex looks down at the floor with empty eyes swaying back and forth.

"I have failed you, but I promise I will not give up on you. You are going through therapy starting tomorrow, and hopefully, after these ten days, we'll see some results. See you tomorrow, Alex."

Doctor Kingsley touches Alex on the shoulder and walks away.

"Butterfly, butterfly."

Alex stops swaying, takes a deep breath, and starts a countdown.

"Ten, nine, eight, seven, six, five, four, three, two, one…"

THE END

ABOUT THE AUTHOR

The author, Rares-Rica Raita, was born on 27 February 1986 in Abrud, a small town in Transylvania, a region of Romania known as a mystical and magical place, the land of vampires and werewolves. He moved to London in 2015, where he worked as an Uber driver and studied marketing. He is still a resident of London, this beautiful city filled with amazing art and literature.

Inspired by his personal experiences, he transformed his life into a captivating psychological thriller and a true masterpiece. He worked as an Uber driver for three years, where he experienced verbal and sexual abuse, but when he fell asleep while driving, he decided to change his career. In 2011, he robbed a petrol station in Romania with a toy gun. That mistake landed him in prison, where he had a weird dream. In his dream, he was in the middle of a raging river, and then a woman told him that he would never leave this place. He was released two months later and placed on probation for eight years. He also did group therapy for a while, in a programme called No More Mr Nice Guy.

Prior to his writing career, he graduated from Roehampton London University in 2021 with a BSc in Marketing. He achieved the TQUK Level 5 Diploma in Education and Training in 2023. Ignoring his credentials, he decided to follow his passion and creativity for writing and painting.

Printed in Great Britain
by Amazon

520125b0-6ca1-4ae4-853b-cea5addee5feR01